Impossible Fate

By Diane Yates

Published by IHeart Publishing

Book Design by IHeart Publishing

 Scripture quotations from The Authorized (King James) Version.

Fiction and Literature: Inspirational
Christian Romantic Suspense
Christian Women's Fiction

ISBN: 978-1-961867-04-8

This story will have you rooting for young love as two likeable characters from different cultures and beliefs learn what it is like to be raised in families with conflicting religious views. I enjoyed the author's storyline with this endearing couple, loving and devoted families and a God that is faithful. I was eager to continue the story with the Drake family. As the story developed, I found my heartbeat pound and had an urgent need to rapidly turn the pages! I am ready for book 3! This quick read will renew your hope in Generation Z. I never wanted it to end. ~ ***Ruth Martin, Director of Library Services, San Diego Christian College***

In her book "Impossible Fate," Diane Yates shows that fate is really the development of events beyond a person's control and yet, regarded as determined by God. And so, what seems Impossible actually becomes possible. This love story is put through so many tests; time; culture; religion; and family. A beautifully written book; helpful in understanding the similarities and differences in others' cultures and faith. With passion, honesty, pain, and respect, this book definitely lights the fire of the soul. ~ ***Aharon Levarko, Israeli Tour Guide***

Can a seven-year-old boy fall in love? At a time when little boys love mud and dislike girls, it's love at first sight when David Drake meets Aliyah Zimmerman on the school bus. Although his parents discount it as puppy love, the relationship blossoms over the coming years. Diane Yates' charming novel, "Impossible Fate" drew me in as I watched David and Aliyah fight insurmountable odds in the forms of religion, distance and parental objections. My pulse raced as I turned each page, wondering how the gap could be bridged. In the end, I closed the book satisfied, yet wanting more. ***~Rochelle Wisoff-Fields, author of PLEASE SAY KADDISH FOR ME, FROM SILT AND ASHES, AS ONE MUST ONE CAN and A STONE FOR THE JOURNEY***

Impossible Fate is a beautiful love story—it captivated me from page one! I rooted for David and Aliyah from the beginning of their friendship and hoped they continued to be together. David, a Christian, and Aliya, a Jew, shared their strong beliefs with each other, not without frustration from their parents; the suspense held my attention the entire time. The story brought my five senses to life—I could *see* each person's individual characteristics; I could *hear* the conversations at the pizza shop; I could *smell* and *taste* the Jewish meals, and I could *feel* Aliya's beautiful, thick, black hair, all as the story unfolded. I now believe in love at first sight! I can't wait for Diane's next book! ***~ Lynette***

Ebberts, Former Director of Media Outreach for the Secretary of Defense, Pentagon.

I really enjoyed reading Impossible Fate by Diane Yates! It is the sequel to Melissa's Fate, but if you haven't yet read the first, that will not hinder you from enjoying the second. When a Christian boy and a Jewish girl grow up as best friends, something wild and crazy could happen, and it does! The drama of the events of 9/11 had me on the edge of my seat! What a plethora of emotions! I couldn't read fast enough! I admire how the details of this historic event and also several cultural celebrations were incorporated into the narrative and appreciate how much research the author must have done to present these with such reality. The best part for me was the weaving of the Gospel message into the storyline. It seemed to be a necessary and inevitable element. Wonderfully written! ~ ***Connie Mellor, retired educator***

Dedication

This book is dedicated to *I Am*, the one and only True God, as I endeavor to love Him with all my heart, soul, mind, and strength, in whose grace I am made perfect. And to my loving husband, who doesn't normally read books but is my #1 fan and editor. A very special thank you to my niece and nephew, Tammi Akers and Darrin Hood, for the amazing trip to Israel last fall. It changed our lives.

We learned so much from our Israeli tour guide, Aharon Levarko. A special thank you to Aharon for his support, endorsement, and for being a fictional character in the book. Only with his expertise and that of a dear friend, author, and artist, Rochelle Wisoff-Fields, did Impossible Fate become a reality. I am thankful for people like Aharon and Rochelle and ministries such as The Jewish Voice and Rabbi Bernis who lift Jesus up unto His own.

Many people walked alongside me during the journey and gave this book wings to fly. Thank you to Ruth Martin, Director of Library Services at San Diego Christian College, for loving David and Aliyah and writing your heartfelt endorsement. My very good friends, Lynette Ebberts and Connie Mellor, inspired and encouraged me every step of the way. You are both near and dear to me. A thank you to my editor, Sherri Stewart, who called it an *amazing book* and to Jocelyn Andersen for her assistance and honest objectivity.

About the cover—not only is the Sea of Galilee in the distance, but my sweet neighbor, Leah, poses as Aliyah. Last but certainly not least, I want to thank you, my readers for picking this book up in the first place. May everyone who reads it be blessed. *Shalom*, Diane

Chapter One

Tuesday, September 11, 2001

Beth Drake waved goodbye to nine-year-old Melissa and seven-year-old David as they climbed aboard the school bus. She picked up the local paper and walked back into the house in time to hear the phone ring. "Hello."

"Hi, Dear." It was Emily, Beth's mom. "Are you sure Phil isn't too busy to have lunch today?"

"Yes. When you finish at the doctor, just give him a call. If he is, he'll let you know."

"Okay, but we'll understand if he's tied up at work."

"No, since you're going to be there anyway for Dad's nephrology appointment, Phil wants to take you to lunch. He mentioned you guys before he left for the city yesterday. He has no relationship with his family, but he loves spending time with the two of you."

Beth felt blessed that her husband loved her parents. After she hung up, she took a shower and dressed before cleaning the kitchen. She was hanging clean dish towels when the phone rang again.

"Beth, are you watching TV?" Tracey, her longtime friend, was panting as if she'd been running.

"No, why?"

"Isn't Jack's office in the World Trade Center?" She squealed, "Turn the TV on!"

As the screen came to life, Beth saw a picture of the tall tower, smoke and flames rising into a troubled sky. She couldn't breathe. "What is it? What happened?"

"A plane crashed into it. A huge airliner."

Beth shook her head and watched in horror as another plane crashed into the second tower. Her heart raced.

Tracey's voice shrieked. "Did you see that?"

Beth gasped. "Yeah, that's a deliberate attack on the World Trade Center."

"Where's Phil's office?" asked Tracey.

Beth didn't answer. All she could think about was Jack, Phil's best friend and attorney; the one who led their fight for custody of Melissa.

"I've got to go." She hung up and dialed Phil but got a busy signal. Jack's office was on the twenty-third floor of the North Tower. Phil's building was several blocks south, but what if he had a meeting with Jack this morning? What if Phil was in that building?

Her mind raced as she dialed and redialed, only to get a strange busy signal. She turned up the volume on the TV. Just this past weekend, Jack and his very pregnant wife, BJ, joined her and Phil and the kids for a backyard barbeque here in West Cornwall, Connecticut.

Is BJ okay? Beth felt the blood drain from her face. People were jumping to their deaths. *Is BJ watching this? She must be sick with worry or worse.* Beth dialed BJ's number but heard the same weird busy signal. They owed much to BJ. She was the private investigator who uncovered evidence for their case in court. Beth and Phil had introduced BJ to Jack, and the rest was history.

Beth kept dialing and redialing number after number as she continued to watch the television.

Tracey rushed through the front door. They hugged and watched in shock as the horrific events unfolded.

"That's Jack's building, isn't it?"

Beth nodded; her eyes glued to the screen. "I can't reach anyone on the phone. Oh, Tracey, what's happening?"

The report they heard next confirmed the nature of the events. A plane crashed into the Pentagon. America was under attack!

Beth's trembling fingers could no longer dial the numbers. Tracey took the phone and continued dialing, to no avail.

Beth suddenly gasped. "Oh no! My parents are in New York today."

The words had scarcely left her mouth when the South Tower started crumbling and a white cloud of dust and debris billowed through the area and down the streets as people ran for cover. The coverage showed rescuers and those they rescued with faces and clothes covered in white.

"Why are they not answering?" Beth shrieked. "Tracey, I have to go. BJ could deliver at any minute. Mom and Dad are there. I don't know about Jack or Phil. Somehow, I have to help."

"You should stay here."

Beth shouldered her purse and pulled the keys off the peg on the wall. "No, I can't stay here."

"Then, I'm coming with you." Tracey grabbed her purse, but Beth raised her hand in front of her.

"I need you to be here when the kids get home.

Please."

~

Tuesday, September eleventh started just like any other Tuesday. Phil Drake arrived at his office building at seven-thirty in the morning and purchased a newspaper at the stand before riding the elevator up to his office. "Good morning, Sandra," he said at the door. "What time is my conference call with Jack?"

"Eight-thirty." His trusted secretary handed him his usual cup of coffee. "And you have a meeting with Mr. Webber at nine-thirty and lunch with your in-laws across town at Mt. Sinai Medical Center."

He glanced out the window at the bay. The sun beamed, ferries moved, boats sailed, the Statue of Liberty still held the torch. All was well in downtown Manhattan. He sat and reviewed the file of the Monaco deal.

At eight-thirty-eight, Sandra put the conference call through. Jack, representing Drake & Webber, was at a law firm in the north tower of the World Trade Center, meeting with Mr. Sutton, the attorney representing the Monaco side of the deal. Phil, Jack, and Mr. Sutton discussed critical negotiations. When Mr. Sutton failed to concede, Phil opened his mouth to object. The line suddenly went dead.

Phil buzzed Sandra, "I lost the call. Can you get them back, please?"

"Of course, sir."

Phil tapped his fingers on his desk, becoming more and more impatient, staring at the phone which remained silent. When the intercom buzzed, he jumped to answer it. "Yes, Sandra."

"Mr. Drake, I can't get an answer at Mr. Sutton's

office, but I'll keep trying."

Phil strode out to Sandra's desk and tapped his thumb on the counter. "What's the holdup?"

Larry Webber burst through the door. "Turn on your TV or radio," he yelled. "It's horrible."

"Keep trying," Phil told Sandra before rushing back to his office with Webber right behind him. He turned on the TV and watched in horror as Tom Kaminski from WCBS reported, "All right, uh, Pat, we are just currently getting a look...at the World Trade Center, we have something that has happened here at the World Trade Center. We noticed flame and an awful lot of smoke from one of the towers of the World Trade Center. We are just coming up on this scene, this is easily three-quarters of the way up...we are...this is...whatever has occurred has just occurred, uh, within minutes and, uh, we are trying to determine exactly what that is. But currently, we have a lot of smoke at the top of the towers of the World Trade Center, we will keep you posted."

Phil stared at Larry, then turned the volume up. "Which building? Tell us which building," he yelled at the TV. His mind instantly went to the meeting taking place at that location. He yelled out to Sandra, "Anything?"

"No, sir."

"Keep trying"

Phil and Larry remained glued to the news coverage. It was about nine o'clock when Phil heard the sound of a plane flying low over their building. In a couple of minutes, the news reported a second plane had crashed into the south face of the South Tower. Panic struck Phil. What in the world was going on? Both buildings had been hit. Jack was in definite danger. He immediately tried Jack's cell but got a strange busy signal.

Phil stared at the television, waiting for any information about the evacuation of the buildings. When he couldn't take it anymore, he said, "Sandra, hold all my calls. Call Beth and let her know I'm going to check on Jack. Tell her I'll call her as soon as I know something."

"But Mr. Drake—"

"And keep trying to call Jack and let me know if you get him."

"Mr. Drake, none of my phone calls are getting out."

"Just keep trying." Phil dashed out the door. On the way down the elevator, his mind raced. One plane could have been a freak accident, but two made it intentional.

Phil stepped outside and stared up. Smoke streaked the sky. Acrid smells permeated the air. Onlookers crowded the sidewalks. Frantic chatter and gasps. He ran when he could and pushed through the crowded areas. Police cars, fire trucks, and ambulances, all with sirens blaring, raced down the streets. Several times Phil had to jump out of the way to allow passage for firemen, dressed in heavy protective suits, boots, helmets, and carrying in tow a myriad of emergency equipment. *What is happening to New York?*

People crowded the sidewalks, some jostling their way toward the scene and others running in the opposite direction. He asked many who were fleeing, "Were you in one of the buildings? Did everyone get out?"

One man shook his head. "Many of us evacuated even though we were told to stay. Firemen are headed up the stairs right now to fight the fire and rescue survivors."

Debris and ash flew through the air as Phil raced

closer to the South Tower. Both buildings had gaping holes and white smoke rising. His eyes burned. The air smelled of fuel. He could feel the heat even from two blocks away.

Police were pushing people away, ordering them to turn back. Phil had to think of something.

"I'm with Waller, Thornton, and Associates," he lied to the officer. "My people are in there. I need to check on them." The officer allowed him to pass, too busy to argue. The farther he went, the more horrific it became—like something out of the worst disaster movie imaginable. Adrenalin kept him moving. Rescuers whisked a lady past him, blood gushing from her forehead, arms, and legs. Others carried a man with soot-covered face and arms, the stench of scorched fabric trailing them to the ambulance.

Screams filled the air. Debris pummeled the ground. Just before he reached the front of the building, he lurched sideways to avoid a sheet of falling plaster. That's when he saw him. A man falling from the sky, landing not thirty feet away. He glanced up. There were others. He squeezed his eyes tight, praying that Jack was okay and this unreal nightmare would soon end.

A strong hand grasped his arm above the elbow. He whirled around to see an officer. "Stop. You can't pass here. You need to evacuate now."

From the sternness in his tone, Phil knew he'd have to find another way to get to Jack's office.

~

Beth wasted no time. Finding it difficult not to speed, she finally gave in and floored the accelerator. How could she calm herself enough to pray? She turned the volume up on the radio. A fourth plane had crashed in a field in Pennsylvania. The FAA grounded all flights, but the radio now said the Port Authority had closed all bridges and tunnels into the city. She wouldn't be able to drive there. Beth turned the car around and headed for the train station.

She dialed Phil's, BJ's, and her parents' cell phone numbers, trying to control her speeding car, but she didn't care. Still, all circuits were busy. Tears threatened. She parked the car and ran into the train station. Once inside, the larger than normal mob slowed her down. The Station's TV's played live coverage of the horrific events and replayed the South Tower's collapse. Her heart raced as she continued to dial Phil's number. Still busy—she sighed.

Beth waited in a long line and, like everyone else, stared at the TV. She shifted from one foot to the other and glanced around the crowd to judge how fast the line moved. Watching live coverage from the screen above, she and others gasped as in front of their eyes, the North Tower collapsed. Beth's breath caught in her throat. Danger closed in from all sides like the plot of a horror movie. This couldn't be happening. *Oh Lord, please let Phil be safe, along with Jack, BJ, Mom and Dad. I pray that Phil was in his office when the planes flew into those buildings.*

Then, on the billboard above, a major change immediately occurred. All routes going into the city were canceled.

Beth dashed back to the car, threw it into gear, and headed south. She would try the ferry. In a frenzy, with phone in hand, she pushed hard on the gas. Dialing and redialing the same numbers, she struggled to keep her eyes on the road long enough to remain safe. She finally called home. Tracey answered.

Beth asked, “Have you heard from Phil or anyone?” Fear tightened her throat, raising the pitch of her voice.

“No, no one. I’ve been trying to reach them all, even your parents, but apparently, the circuits can’t handle the volume of calls.”

“I couldn’t take a train. I’m going to try to catch a ferry.”

“Beth, you should come back home.”

“No, I have to find my parents and make sure Phil, Jack, and BJ are okay.” Her car swayed over the line just as a truck appeared from over a hill. Its horn blared and Beth swerved into the right lane. “I have to go, Tracey. Call me if you hear anything.” She didn’t wait for Tracey to respond. For the first time, she placed the phone in its holder. No sense in her children losing their mother while she was trying to confirm everyone else’s well-being.

Forty-five minutes later, she finally reached the ferry in New London. It was easy to find a parking space, and she ran inside and up to the counter. “Are there any ferries going into Manhattan?” Two TV’s played the disaster of the morning’s events. “I need a ticket on the first ferry to Long Island.”

“Honey, there are no ferries going anywhere. All ferry service has been suspended.”

Beth stared at the ferry clerk. This couldn’t be happening. “Where’s the nearest helicopter?”

“They’ve shut down all air traffic. Nothing’s going in or out of the city.”

Beth backed away slowly. It was as if the breath had been knocked out of her. She could think of no other way to get there, to reach the people she loved, to know they were okay.

The TV showed the White House and the Capitol evacuating earlier and reported they had been targeted. She paused a moment to listen. President Bush had been at a school in Florida where he addressed the nation earlier but now was on board Air Force One. Location unknown. This was crazy. Fear gripped her soul.

~

David listened to his sister talking to her friend in the seat behind him as the bus followed the curve up the hill. It came to a stop at a new driveway where it had never stopped before.

"Why? I just want to go to school. I want to see Chad and the other kids. I don't want to stop anymore."

He sighed, but when he saw a girl outside the window, he stopped rotating the arm of his miniature Bob the Builder figure. She must be new because he'd never seen her before. He watched as she climbed aboard. Her hair, a thick mass of black curls, extended down her back and was pulled into clips on the sides. He recognized her Bear in the Big Blue House backpack.

The bus only had a few empty seats, but as she walked down the aisle, she attempted to sit in one spot after another. One girl shook her head when she eyed the seat next to her. Toby put his backpack in the seat when she started to sit there. She looked like she might cry as she continued toward the back and the one empty seat next to him.

He stuffed Bob in his pocket and stared out the window as she sat down. They rode in silence. As the bus pulled into the school drive, he ventured a glance at her. She pulled her Bear in the Big Blue House backpack over her shoulders and smiled, exposing two front teeth that had grown in only halfway. Her eyes were dark brown, and she had the prettiest olive skin. Embarrassed, he jerked his head away.

David nodded toward Mrs. Martin, his second-grade teacher, and headed to his desk behind Chad. While she wrote September 11, 2001, on the chalkboard, the principal appeared at the door with the new girl from the bus.

"Mrs. Martin, you have a new student. This is Aliyah Zimmerman," the principal announced.

"Hi, Aliyah." His teacher touched the girl's shoulder and turned to the class. "Everyone, let's make Aliyah feel welcome." Mrs. Martin showed the new girl to her desk—the empty one right behind David.

He wasn't sure why he felt so shy, especially over a girl. The only one he liked was his sister and that was only when she was being nice to him or he wanted something of hers.

"Can you come over this evening?" Chad asked while they proceeded in single file to the lunchroom, but David didn't want to talk. It was as if his voice had left him. Chad turned and punched his shoulder lightly. "What's wrong with you?"

"Nothing," David protested a little too loudly.

That caught Mrs. Martin's attention. "Chad, David, not a day passes that I don't have to call you two out." She placed her finger over her lips.

David sat down next to Chad as he always did. The new girl, Aliyah, was still wandering, lunch tray in hand, looking uncomfortable. None of the girls invited her to sit with them. For some inexplicable reason, David scooted over and made room for her.

Her face lit up with a broad smile. She sat down and

opened her milk. "So, what's your name?" she asked Chad.

After David's friend answered, she turned to him. "And what's yours?"

His cheeks warmed and his palms started sweating. He opened his mouth, but nothing came out.

Aliyah stuck a French fry in her mouth and shook her head. "You don't have a name, or you don't want to talk to me?"

Chad started laughing. David hung his head. *Why did I let her sit here?* "Both," he blurted. "I mean, Da…David, and I don't want to talk."

She shrugged. "Suit yourself." She turned towards Chad. "You read really good, Chad. David does, too, but he doesn't want to talk to me."

David stared at his plate and regretted everything from the moment she walked in the lunchroom. For the rest of their lunch break, Chad and Aliyah laughed and talked.

On the way back to the classroom, they passed several rooms with televisions blaring, but those were in the older classes. Their room didn't have one. As soon as they had settled back at their desks, Mrs. Martin announced, "Boys and girls, something happened today in New York City and at the Pentagon. Some of the other kids might be talking about it. It involves planes. You can talk with your parents this evening and ask them any questions, okay?"

That afternoon, David climbed aboard the bus first.

When Aliyah started down the aisle, she eyed the spot beside him. "Can I sit with you?"

He nodded and placed his Bob the Builder backpack on the floor. She removed her Bear in the Big Blue

House and set it next to his. "Why don't kids like me?" She looked straight at him. "Why don't you like me?"

David shrugged. "I didn't say I didn't like you." *Boy, was she pushy.*

"But you won't talk to me. Is it because I'm Jewish?"

"You're what?"

"You know—are you American or Muslim or Buddhist or Christian? I'm Jewish."

He understood American and Christian but didn't know about the others. "What's Jewish?"

"My mom says it's who we are." She wrinkled her eyebrows and squinted. "Like the color of our skin. Anyway, we believe in God or Adonai."

He nodded. "We believe in God, too. I'm Christian."

The gleam in her eyes dimmed. "Oh," she said. She took out a piece of notebook paper from her backpack and a pencil. "Do you know your phone number?"

His mom had made him memorize that and his address a long time ago. "Of course."

When he didn't say more, she lifted her pencil from her paper and glanced up at him, sighing. "Well, are you going to tell me or what?"

Chapter Two

After turning the car around, hopeless and defeated, Beth called Tracey. "Anything, yet?"

"No, nothing. Did you make it to the ferry?"

"Yes, but they're not running. Nothing is running."

"That's probably because they're trying to get everyone out of Manhattan, not let people in. Come home."

"I'm on my way back now."

"Um…Beth…"

"Oh, Tracey, I have to know."

"Beth…I just saw—"

"What? What did you just see?" Beth was frantic, fearing the worst.

"I think it was Phil, walking on the street away from the Trade Center. I'm not sure, though. His hair was covered with ash and his clothes were white. A police officer was turning people away."

"Oh, I pray you're right." Beth's hopes soared.

"It looked like him, but I could be wrong."

"I'll be home soon."

She had no sooner hung up than the phone rang. At the sound of Phil's voice, relief washed over Beth like warm water in a cold shower. "Phil, thank God."

"Beth, I've been trying to call you." He sounded strange, like he was in shock. They all were.

"Are you okay?"

"Yes…yes…I'm fine." He sounded breathless and frantic. "I tried to walk to Jack's building… make sure he was alright…see if I could help in some way…but, it collapsed before I could get there. I don't know, Beth."

Phil's voice cracked. "I don't know…if he made it."

"Had you talked to him this morning?"

"Yes. We were in the middle of a conference call when the phone went dead."

"Oh, no. That's not good. I mean—"

"I know."

"Have you heard from BJ? I can't get through. I'm worried about her and the baby. How she's taking this? If she went into labor, I don't think she could get an ambulance."

"I didn't think, Beth. I didn't think about BJ. I'll try to check on her."

"And my parents. Have they called you?"

"Oh, no. That's right. Are they here?" His voice raised an octave.

"I assume. I talked to Mom this morning, but I can't reach her cell now."

"None of the phones are working. I'm lucky I made it through to you."

"I tried to catch a train, but they're canceled. I drove to the ferry at New London, but—"

"Beth—"

"The ferries aren't running. The helicopters aren't flying—"

"Beth—"

"Phil, how can I get there?" Never had she felt so trapped. She needed to be in New York.

"Beth, you can't get into the city. They're evacuating lower Manhattan now. It's crazy pandemonium here. Stay there with the kids."

"But I have to find my parents and I want to be there for BJ."

"I know, but you've never seen anything like this.

None of us have."

There was silence on the line. Had she lost him? "Phil? Are you still there?"

"I'm here. What was the name of the doctor your dad was seeing? I'll look for them and I'll make it to BJ, too. And I'll keep searching for any news on Jack."

"I wish I could be there with you." Beth told him the doctor's name and assured him she would return home. "Phil, be careful. You know I love you."

"I know. And I you, my love."

Hanging up was hard for her to do. Once the connection was lost, there was no telling when she would hear his voice again. Trusting in God, and Phil, she would stop trying to reach her parents and BJ for a while. Still, she kept glancing at her phone and wishing with all her heart it would ring with comforting news. She finally drove into her driveway, still worried but relieved and thankful that her husband was okay.

~

Phil returned to his office, washed his face, changed his clothes, grabbed the car keys out of his white debris-covered pants and walked through his recently evacuated office building. In record time, he drove out of the parking garage two blocks away and headed north to Mt. Sinai Medical Center.

The intersection of Pearl and Broad Street was blocked off, but he drove between the barriers and continued. As he got closer, he had to pull over more than once to allow emergency vehicles to pass. He finally reached within a block and parked the car on the right-hand side of the street. It wasn't a parking space but wasn't in anyone's way. He hurried to the entrance, rushed inside, and stopped at the directory. That's when he heard a familiar voice.

"Phil?"

It was Emily, Beth's mom, and Walter right behind her. "Mom, Dad? You're here."

"We decided to stay here since we couldn't get out of the city and had no place to go," Walter said.

"That was smart." Phil felt relieved to find them both so easily. He loved his in-laws more than most. They were warm and caring; nothing like his parents. "Beth's been trying to call you."

Emily wrinkled her forehead. "We've been trying to call her, but my phone's not working." Walter put his arm around his wife who seemed to be reacting much the same as Beth.

Phil tried to sound calm, hoping it would help Emily relax. "She's okay. I talked to her earlier. Everyone's trying to call in or out. The circuits are overloaded. It's hard to reach anyone."

He drove them to his apartment on Fifth Avenue by Central Park and shared about his events of the day. "I have to go, but I'll be back as soon as possible," he told them. "Will you guys be okay?"

"We'll be fine, Son," Walter said. "You find your friends. We'll be praying right here."

As he left, he thought about how lucky he was to have in-laws like Walter and Emily and to have found Beth. She'd shown him the value of life, love, and faith, things he would never have found without her.

One by one, he traveled to the hospitals in the area to check for Jack and BJ. When he checked New York Methodist Hospital, he was told BJ had been admitted to Labor and Delivery on the second floor.

He rushed to her room. She was huffing and sweaty

and reached for him when he entered.

"Phil! Phil, thank God you've come."

He rushed to her side and took her hand in his. She squeezed hard, gritted her teeth, and then screamed. He caressed her forehead, trying to calm her.

When her pain subsided, she pleaded. "Have you heard from Jack?"

"No, but I'm sure he's fine." Phil wished he were sure, but he didn't want her worrying.

"Oh, Phil, if he's okay, why doesn't he call?"

"The phones aren't working."

The nurse chased Phil out of the room, saying she needed to check her patient's progress.

"No," BJ objected. "My husband was in the Twin Towers, and I don't know if he's all right. Phil's a close friend and I need him here." She wasn't requesting, but rather demanding that he stay.

~

Tracey had stayed a while but then had to leave. When the kids arrived home, Melissa asked Beth questions about the attacks, but once she heard her father was okay, she went upstairs to play. David seemed preoccupied, a blessing in disguise. Beth left the TV on all evening, hoping for any news. She was unable to reach BJ, Jack, or her parents despite many attempts. She willed the phone to ring and when it finally did, she rushed to answer.

"Hello?"

"Um," the voice was that of a little girl. "Is David home?"

"Yes, but he can't talk right now."

Beth couldn't remember if she said goodbye or not. It was imperative that her line remain open. The next hours passed slowly, and the phone only rang twice more. Each time, Beth's heart skipped a beat, but each time it was the same little girl. The last time she called, frustrated Beth. "Please don't call back again tonight. I'm expecting other calls."

"Mom, what's for dinner?" David hollered.

"Hm?" Beth turned to see that Melissa and David were in the kitchen doorway. *Dinner? How can I possibly eat dinner?* She hadn't eaten anything since breakfast, nor did she want anything, but the kids needed to eat. "Why don't we order pizza?" Lucky for her, Pizza Hut had recently opened a new store in Cornwall, and they delivered.

"Yay!" The kids jumped up and down at the mention of one of their favorites. "I want cheese," Melissa chimed in.

"But I want pepperoni," David objected.

"We'll order both with salads and soda."

Beth monitored the news, her thoughts unsettled. She knew many had died, including firefighters, policemen, and other first responders. She prayed for the safety of Jack, BJ, and her mother and father.

Were they at war? President Bush had addressed the nation from an Air Force base in Louisiana earlier, but now he was somewhere in Nebraska. That was all she knew. All anyone knew.

Her phone remained silent the rest of the evening. She tucked the kids into bed without baths and resumed her spot in front of the TV screen.

At eight-thirty, President Bush addressed the nation from the oval office.

He said the acts were "evil, despicable acts of terror" and that we would "stand together to win the war against terrorism."

The clock struck ten, but Beth couldn't possibly sleep. When the phone rang, she answered it in less than a second. "Hello?"

"Beth," he sounded winded.

"Phil?"

"I've been with BJ. She had an eight-pound baby boy, and he's just perfect."

"Really? When?" A strange mix of emotions filled her—joy for BJ, anxiety for her parents and Jack.

"Uh, just now. Well, ten minutes ago."

"How is she?"

"She's fine. They gave her something to help her sleep."

"Phil—"

"I took your parents to the apartment, but I haven't found Jack yet."

She took a deep breath and released it slowly. "I'm sorry, Phil." Her eyes filled with tears.

There was silence before he responded. "Just keep praying, okay?"

She wiped at the tears and cleared her throat. "Always. Call me if you hear anything. Give BJ my love."

"Beth, I wish you were here. I miss you so much. You're my whole world, and today I saw how easily one's world can change."

The tears flowed freely now, and she couldn't prevent choking up. "Oh, Phil, I miss you. How I wish I were there and could hold you in my arms." She did want to hold him, but she really longed for his arms to hold her.

"Try to get some sleep, my love. I'll call you in the

morning."

She nodded, blotting at the tears with a tissue and sniffing. "Phil, I love you."

"I love you, honey."

~

Phil hung up and was heading back toward BJ's room when a nurse approached him.

"Were you the one asking about Jack Thornton?"

Phil's heart rose to his throat. "Yes."

"Come with me." Along the way, the nurse informed him Jack had been brought to the ER about an hour ago. He had helped people out of the North Tower before going into the South Tower to assist the rescue efforts there. "It seems as the Tower collapsed, he was trapped under debris for the better part of the day. By the time they uncovered him, he had several broken ribs and a broken right femur."

Even though Jack was bruised and bandaged, the sight of him overwhelmed Phil when he entered his room. "Jack," Phil exclaimed. "You're a sight for sore eyes."

Jack's voice was barely a whisper, and he winced in pain. "You mean I'm a sore for anybody's eyesight!"

"You're a hero from what I've heard. I'm looking at an amazing hero."

"Can you call BJ? She's probably out of her mind with worry."

"No need. She's here. Gave birth to an eight-pound baby boy that looks just like you, poor kid."

Jack's eyes widened and he tried to move, but Phil gently placed his hand on his shoulder. "No, you rest. Your family's not going anywhere."

Chapter Three

The next day, David dressed for school in record time and ran downstairs, eager to catch the bus. His mom was on the phone, talking to his grandma.

"Mom," Beth said, "you and Dad can stay at Phil's as long as you need."

On his way out, David felt a tug on his shirt, twisting him around. Even though she still held the receiver to her ear, his mom managed to kiss his forehead and hand him his lunch money. She mouthed the words "love you" and continued with her call. "Don't go home until the trains are running and the crowds have thinned out."

David boarded the bus with Melissa like always, but never had he been this thrilled to go to school. He'd left Bob the Builder lying on his desk, but he'd tucked inside his backpack the Bratz doll his sister had placed in a bag to be donated. *Maybe Aliyah would like it.* As the bus proceeded along the winding roads, he couldn't wait to reach her stop. And then, there she was.

He watched her run to the bus with her backpack. She wore a white shirt and gray pleated skirt that resembled the one she wore yesterday. Her long black hair was partly braided and draped like a headband surrounding the rest of her soft curls.

Aliyah headed down the aisle without trying to sit anywhere else, smiling from ear to ear. His heart pounded and he smiled back when she sat down beside him. She put her backpack on the floor. "I tried to call you. Was that your mom who answered?"

He nodded. "Yeah, it was probably her."

"Wow. She's mean." Aliyah made a face, gritting her teeth, the corners of her mouth turned down.

"What? Not my mom. You must have called a wrong number."

"No, I didn't. She said you couldn't talk and then told me not to call back."

David frowned. It didn't sound like his mom. Why would she do that? Then he remembered her strange behavior yesterday. "I think she was waiting to hear from my grandma and grandpa. They were in New York where the planes crashed into the buildings."

Aliyah nodded. "Oh, yeah, that was terrible. My grandparents live there and also my aunts, uncles, and cousins. Do your grandparents live there, too?"

"No. They live in Hartford but were in New York yesterday. My Dad's parents live there, but I've never seen them."

"What do you mean you've never seen them? Why not?"

David shrugged. He didn't know. The bus turned into the school drive, and he hadn't even given her the doll yet. They both grabbed their things. While walking down the aisle, one of the older boys knocked David's bag out of his hands. When it fell, some of its contents spilled out, including the doll. David struggled to tuck it back in.

Tommy shouted, "Ooh. David plays with dolls." The boys started laughing.

"No, I don't."

Melissa chimed in next, and things went from bad to worse. "David, that's my Bratz doll. You stole it from me."

"I didn't steal it. You were giving it away," he protested.

As Aliyah watched, he felt the heat in his cheeks, even though Melissa admitted he was right.

All the boys from first through fifth grade chanted, "David plays with dolls. David plays with dolls."

Aliyah pushed Tommy backward, and he fell to the floor. The chanting stopped as the boys stared at Tommy. Aliyah grabbed the doll. "It's mine. David gave it to me." She turned to David, and his world righted itself as she smiled. "Thank you, I've been wanting one," she continued, "but I can carry it myself if all these juveniles are going to have conniption fits."

She tossed her hair back and, with her head held high, marched away and down the steps.

David smirked, took a deep breath, pushing his chest out as he left the bus. She was something. And he couldn't wait until lunchtime.

~

Phil sat by the fire. It was four am and he was unable to sleep. It had become a pattern since 9/11. He'd wake up in a sweat. Sometimes he remembered his nightmare, other times, not. This time in the morning allowed him to reflect on God. Ten years ago, he would never have imagined his life as it was today. For that, he was thankful. Because of Beth and her family, he'd come to know Jesus personally and the difference He could make in one's life. His home with Beth and the children contained a peace that he'd never known before. Still, the attacks on the World Trade Center made him realize how precious life was.

Lately, he couldn't get his mind off his family, the one of his birth—his father, the distant, apathetic, incapable-of-love sperm donor to his existence. His mother was always more interested in their affluent lifestyle and treasured travel and possessions more than her offspring. His parents were quite a pair. With his father's apparent dislike of Beth, Phil hadn't cared if he ever saw him again. And then, 9/11 happened, making eternity a reality for so many right before his eyes.

Phil thought about the visit from his brother the other day. Charles Drake was only two years older than Phil and the middle son of Augustine Drake, III, founder of the Drake Aerospace dynasty. Daniel was the oldest. Both of Phil's brothers followed in their father's footsteps; both sat on the board of Drake Aerospace Industries.

It was Charles who had surprised Phil in the middle of the day on September sixth, by bursting into his office before Sandra could announce him. "Phillip, we need to talk," he'd demanded.

Phil stood and they shook hands more like businessmen than brothers. "This is a surprise. What brings you to my office, Charles?"

His brother was a little taller, leaner, and perhaps more determined than all three of the Drake boys. He picked up the frame on Phil's desk and stared at Beth and the kids. "Nice picture."

Phil removed it from his hands and placed it back on

the desk. "Thank you." What was his brother up to?

"Are you happy, Phil? Really?"

Phil didn't know where his brother was going with this, but he was happy to defend his life. "I am. Everything's pretty perfect."

Charles laughed. "How can that be? I mean, you live in a Podunk town in the middle of nowhere in a shack of a house, married to a woman lacking all the social graces. No wonder you don't ever want to bring her around."

Phil pointed his finger at himself. "*I* don't want to be around. Beth has more class in her little finger than all the Drakes and Hamiltons put together, but you would never understand that."

Charles sat on the sofa and draped his arm along the back of it, making himself at home. One might have thought it was his office instead of Phil's. He crossed his legs and brushed a piece of lint off his pants "It's time we put this feud behind us."

"I'm not feuding, I'm just not participating. My home is full of love, laughter, and celebration. We never had that growing up."

Charles leaned forward. "Dad has cancer. It's in his lungs. They're going to do chemo and radiation, but I don't think there's a cure." He continued with a chuckle. "I'll always remember him, smoking a cigar—the finest Cuban variety, of course."

Phil didn't have a comeback. He could think of nothing to say. His lack of feeling concerned him. After all, this was his father they were talking about.

~

Beth awoke and glanced at the clock beside the bed. Phil's side was vacant. She stepped into her slippers, slipped on her robe, and went downstairs. Light came from the study. She paused at the door, watching her husband as he sat in his chair, staring at the fire. Beth's heart melted. A cloud had loomed over him since that tragic day, a month ago. There didn't seem to be anything she could do to help. Beth cleared her throat and joined him. She gently massaged his shoulders. "Couldn't sleep?"

He covered one of her hands with his own. "I'm sorry. Did my absence wake you?"

Beth leaned over and kissed his forehead. "I always miss you when you're not there." She sat in the other chair and eyed him. "What is it, Phil? Tell me."

He stared at the fire. "My brother came to my office a few weeks ago."

"Which brother?" She didn't know anything about either of his brothers except their names. Phil avoided talking about the Drakes.

"Charles." Phil's eyes met hers. "My father has cancer."

Beth touched his arm. "Oh, honey. I'm sorry."

"I don't feel anything." Phil shook his head. "I...don't...feel anything, Beth."

She wished she knew what to say, but his family was a mystery to her. They were not at all like hers. All she could do was move to the side of his chair and wrap her arms around his neck as the two of them stared into the fire.

"Charles said I should go to the annual Hamilton feast for Thanksgiving."

"Do you want to go?" Beth knew little about this event. His mother's side of the family, the Hamiltons, met every year at Thanksgiving. All the family members purchased tickets to attend, and an obscene check amount would be donated to that year's charity. It sounded good, except Phil said their altruism was just for image.

"No." Phil peered up at Beth and frowned. "but maybe I'm supposed to reach out. I've been praying about it."

"I've often wondered about that, too. Perhaps, you should make an effort, especially now."

He stood and pulled her into his arms. "I don't want to subject you to them. Nor Melissa and David, for that matter. My family can be merciless."

His embrace warmed her like no fire could. She kissed him softly before smiling. "Your wife and kids are up to the challenge. We're a team. We can take it."

His eyes twinkled. "If anyone could, it would be you." He kissed her, and she thrilled at his touch as he pulled her even closer.

~

Beth was making pumpkin cookies when David sat on a stool at the island and grabbed one off the plate. "Mm," he raised his eyebrows and murmured. "Not bad."

"Not bad? I'll have you know this is one of my grandma's famous recipes, and they're darn good." Beth paused, expecting David to have a comeback, but he stared at the island and half frowned. "Is something wrong?" she asked after a few moments of silence.

He shook his head, still thinking. "Mom?"

"Yes?"

"What's Jewish?"

"Why do you ask?"

"Oh, it's nothing."

David started to climb down, but Beth grabbed his

hand, tugging him back to his spot. "Yes, it is. Let's have it. What's going on?"

"It's Aliyah. Her mom doesn't want her to play with me because she's Jewish."

Beth wiped her hands on her apron and sat on the stool next to him. She wasn't sure what to say. Her little man, dressed in blue jeans, a t-shirt, and sneakers captured her heart, especially after getting his hair cut this afternoon. "Aliyah? That's the little girl we met at the shopping mall the other day?"

He nodded.

She was an adorable child, but Beth had no idea she was Jewish. "Really, her mom said that?"

David nodded again still frowning.

Beth handed him a cookie, grabbed one herself, and took a bite. She knew her little boy liked this young girl immensely, so she carefully considered her words. "You know how we go to a Christian church and we believe that Jesus is the savior or Messiah. The Jews don't believe that Jesus is the Messiah."

Phil walked into the kitchen at that precise moment. "Well, it's more than that. It's a culture, a people." He set his briefcase down and eyed the cookies. "Yum."

Beth always thrilled at the sight of her husband after a long week of him being in New York and her holding the fort down at home. He bent to kiss her and wrapped his arms around her as they each enjoyed a longer kiss.

"Yuck!" David squealed and slid off the stool, leaving them alone.

Beth stood, enjoying Phil's warm embrace. The weeks were long, and she lived for these moments of reunion, longed for nighttime when they'd be alone in each other's arms. When the kiss ended, she whispered through misty eyes, "I missed you so much."

"I know. Me, too. I'm working on something…well, I'll tell you later."

"No, tell me now."

He shook his head and grabbed a cookie. "What was that all about with David?"

She took some of the cooking utensils to the sink. "He has this little girl at school whom he's friends with; only her mother has told her she can't play with him because he's not Jewish."

Phil's eyes widened as he chewed. "Seriously?" he said. "Hmm."

"Yeah," Beth sighed.

"Well, we'll have to give that some thought. Where's Melissa?"

"Upstairs in her room." Beth opened the dishwasher.

Phil loosened his tie. "I'm going upstairs to change." He kissed her again, lightly. "I'll check in on her and David."

Beth watched Phil leave the room with a smile on her face, remembering how he had been afraid of failing as a dad. He hadn't wanted to be like his father. No dad could love their children more than Phil.

~

It was the last day of school before Thanksgiving. David sat with Aliyah just as he had ever since her first day, 9/11, watching her play Tetris on his Gameboy. Every day he snuck it out of the house in his backpack because he knew how much she liked it. She said her parents didn't let her play with things like that. Mostly, it seemed, she didn't play much at all. Her mom was helping her read something called the Torah. He didn't understand, but he didn't have to. She had become his best friend, so they played on the bus, at recess, and sat together at lunch.

Her head bobbed along with the motions of the buttons on the game and he laughed at her. “No, no, no!” she cried out as she died.

David laughed. “My turn,” and he tried to take the handheld game away.

She moved it away from his reach. “Let me have one more turn, please?” she pleaded with him with a little smile. “Please?”

He sighed, but he liked it when she smiled. “Okay.”

The bus pulled into the school, and she gave the game back to him. While he was tucking it away, she slipped out of the seat, flicked her hair to the back, and laughed. “Come on, Dave, we don’t want to be late.”

“Don’t call me that.” He acted mad, but he knew she was teasing. She always called him Dave when she wanted a reaction. “My name is David.”

They scuffled down the aisle.

Chapter Four

Thanksgiving Day 2001

Beth, Phil, and the kids stayed in the city the night before the Annual Hamilton Feast. Beth meticulously brushed, curled, and styled Melissa's hair. She looked adorable in her long, silk, amethyst formal, trimmed with a burnt-orange velvet ribbon. Her shoes possessed a hint of a heel and tapped as she walked.

Beth had given David strict orders to sit on the sofa and not to wrinkle his tailor-made suit or scuff his shined shoes. Phil had tied David's burnt-orange tie earlier. When Melissa joined him, they made a perfect picture, but pictures would have to wait until they arrived at Hampton Hall.

With a last-minute appraisal of her looks in the mirror, Beth hoped to ease her nerves. Her coordinated orange gown, accented with silk embroidered amethyst doves and heels of the same color, matched her amethyst velvet ribbon, accentuating her tiny waist. Her hair piled on top of her head and the diamonds around her neck made her the picture of elegance, but that didn't put her qualms at ease. Nevertheless, when Phil finished tying his tie and turned to look at his family, Beth smiled, summoning all her strength to appear calm and confident. It was important for Phil to believe they would be fine, despite what transpired.

Beth had only seen Phil's father twice, the day billionaire Augustine Drake tried to pay her, a common person, to leave his son alone, and again on the day when she and Phil went to tell her parents about their marriage and Melissa's birth. She had prayed for him since finding out about his illness, but she was sure he wouldn't be thrilled to see her. Maybe meeting his grandchildren would defrost his heart of stone.

As Beth's memories surfaced, she was thankful she and Phil had found each other again and were reunited with Melissa, even if it had been twenty months after Melissa's birth and adoption. She was thankful God had fixed all the wrongs of her past and gave her this glorious family and life.

Phil glanced at Beth, lines furrowing between his brows. "Shall we get this party started?"

Beth's eyes widened and she took a deep breath. "Lead the way, Maestro. Come along, children."

The four of them drove out of Manhattan and took Interstate 495 to the Hamptons.

"Daddy," Melissa asked, "Why haven't we met your mom and dad before?"

Phil shot Beth a look. "It just hasn't worked out until now, honey."

David spoke next. "What are we supposed to call them?"

Phil stared at the road ahead, not answering at first. "I think you should call them Grandfather and

Grandmother Drake. How does that sound?"

"Okay."

Beth smiled at Phil when he glanced at her for affirmation. Inside, her stomach was turning flip-flops. She had never met "Grandmother Drake." What should she call Augustine and Louise Drake? Mom and Dad? She wouldn't dare. How about, Mother and Father Drake? Nope, she didn't have confidence for that either. There was no other choice but Mr. and Mrs. Drake.

Even though the drive took over an hour, before Beth knew it, they were there. With her heart racing and palms sweating, she checked her children after exiting the car and straightened David's tie. Then, she followed her husband, holding Melissa's and David's hands as they walked on the red carpet past the easel with the sign that read: *Welcome to the 30th Annual Hamilton Feast.* They entered the vast foyer with its magnificent crystal chandelier and left their coats with the hatcheck girl, then proceeded straight ahead into the Ruby Ballroom.

An orchestra was playing "Moonlight in Vermont." Couples mingled around tall white linen-clad tables with flickering candles, clinking champagne glasses, and lost in conversation. Children scampered through French doors that led to a garden or solarium. So, this was Phil's mother's family, the Hamiltons.

A man approached them. "Phil,"—he held out his hand—"I'm glad you decided to join us this year. It's been too long."

Phil grinned. "Perhaps. Daniel, this is my wife, Beth. Beth, this is my older brother, Daniel."

As Beth lifted her hand, Daniel took it and placed a kiss on it. She smiled. "It's nice to meet you at last. And, I agree, it's been too long—"

Phil interrupted. "And this is Melissa and David."

Before Daniel could respond, a tall brunette joined them. She was Daniel's wife, Charlotte, and they had an eight-year-old son out in the solarium. After Charles and his wife, Sophia, joined them, the children were encouraged to adjourn to the solarium with the younger Hamilton offspring, but Beth stayed with her children until she knew they were comfortable.

Beth froze as she walked back into the Ruby Ballroom. She recognized the older gentleman standing on Phil's left side, but a middle-aged, sophisticated lady stood on his right. Her diamond earrings sparkled as she laughed, and her cream-colored gown revealed her slender form and contrasted with her soft brown hair. Beth took a deep breath and forced one foot in front of the other.

Phil stepped forward and placed his arm around her. "Beth, this is my mother, Louise, and I believe you've met my father." Despite her age, Mrs. Drake was a strikingly beautiful woman.

Beth acknowledged Mr. Drake with a nod and would have greeted Mrs. Drake with pleasantries but refused to speak until the older woman had finished surveying her from head to toe. When her mother-in-law's eyes met hers, she smiled and offered a handshake. "It's very nice to finally meet you, Mrs. Drake."

"Yes, dear. Same here." The corners of her mouth barely curved upward, and her voice remained flat. "I suppose the children are here somewhere."

"Yes, Mother, they're in the garden," Phil answered.

"I'll see them soon enough since we're all dining at the same table." She turned her attention to Phil. "I believe they have us; that is, your dad and me, the four of you, and Charles and Sophia all seated together."

"Phil, be sure and speak to your Aunt Kate," Mr. Drake ordered.

"Yes, Dad, I'll make the rounds."

"Yes, and be sure to stop by your grandparents' table," his mother added.

Phil grabbed two glasses of champagne from a passing waiter and handed one to Beth while raising his eyebrows. The orchestra played a cue and the leader announced the commencement of dinner. The family headed into the Emerald Ballroom for the feast.

Oh, great. I wonder how awkward it's going to be sitting at the same table with my arch- nemesis and the rest of Phil's family. I can do this.

Phil pushed Beth's chair in for her, Melissa sat next to her, then David. Next to David sat Mr. Drake and Mrs. Drake, which put Beth directly opposite her mother-in-law.

The food was delicious, but the conversation dragged. Beth noted that Sofia called Mrs. Drake, Louise. Mr. Drake seemed almost human when he interacted with the others, but he didn't address her at all.

It was during the main course when David, who was sitting next to his grandfather, said, "Grandfather Drake, do you make airplanes? I mean your company?"

The reserved gentleman answered, "Yes, David, it does, all kinds."

"How many kinds are there?"

"David, finish your meal," Phil instructed.

"No, Phillip. It's okay." Then Mr. Drake turned to his grandson. "We make military planes, space shuttles, drones—"

"What are drones?" David interrupted with

exuberant curiosity.

Mr. Drake loosened up and became animated with an elevated voice and hand gestures. "They are the finest technology money can buy and the key to future military endeavors. Drones are unmanned planes that fly remotely."

David gasped with raised eyebrows.

Mr. Drake turned to Phil. "Why have you not scheduled a time for my grandson to visit his grandfather?" Then he leaned closer to David. "You come by my office. I'll show you these marvels myself and explain all about them."

"Dad," Charles interjected, "I don't think taking children to the facility is a good idea."

"Why not, Uncle Charles?" Melissa asked.

He didn't look at Melissa, but rather at his father and then at Phil. "Because that technology is still top secret."

"Nonsense," bellowed Augustine. "It's not like a seven-year-old boy is going to steal the blueprints. He can come if I say he can."

There it was—a smile from Louise Drake when her husband squeezed David's shoulder. The two gestures were more than Beth had hoped for. By the time they finished dessert, Beth and Sofia had exchanged a couple words, and Mrs. Drake even told Beth about her tea party at Bloomingdale's in December to raise money for the children's hospital.

As the day came to an end, Phil, Charles, and Daniel were talking with their father in a serious-looking conversation by the table in the corner.

Sophia and Charlotte hovered together some twenty feet away from Beth. While approaching them, she overheard Sophia ask Charlotte, "What do you suppose they're talking about?" Beth stopped in her tracks.

"They're probably discussing his treatment," Charlotte replied. "They're supposed to start it next week."

Sophia squinted her eyes. "They'd better be talking about the will. And making sure Phil isn't in it. You should have seen the way that little one was sucking up to Augustine during dinner."

"Sophia," Charlotte scolded, but neither of them noticed Louise, who had snuck in from the side door and stood behind them.

"Now, girls. Don't you go worrying yourselves about the will. You'll get your fair shares."

Beth, who stood unnoticed, rolled her eyes and wished to be far, far away from here.

~

Christmas music played on the stereo while Beth, Melissa, and David decorated the tree with the family ornaments they had accumulated over the past years—beautiful store-bought ones, others made in school, and homemade ornaments. Phil brought in a bowl of popcorn, and both the kids busied themselves stringing the kernels.

"Who wants hot cocoa?" Beth asked.

After all the "I do's," Beth made cocoa for four. David joined her and sat on a barstool at the island. Without saying anything, he stared at the fruit bowl of oranges. Beth could tell her young man was thinking. She went to touch his nose with her finger, but he moved out of her reach.

"Mom," he protested.

She set his cup down in front of him. "What are you thinking about so intensely?"

He took a drink, leaving a chocolate mustache. "You know how you said you and Dad were made for each other."

"Um-hum." Beth wiped the counter.

"Well…how old do you have to be to fall in love?" Beth glanced at Phil on the sofa and stifled a chuckle, but Melissa broke into a hilarious roar as she reached for her cocoa.

"What do you know about love? You're just a second grader."

"Melissa." Beth shook her head, and Phil summoned his daughter to hang the star on the tree.

Beth studied her seven-year-old son. "I guess that depends. Why do you ask?"

David stared at the countertop. Then, he slowly raised his eyes. "Because…I think I'm…in love with Aliyah."

Phil and Beth looked at each other. She suppressed the giggle that was bubbling up, but little David remained stone-cold serious. This scene would be forever etched in her memory. She'd never seen anything cuter. Beth chose her words carefully and was thankful that Melissa busied herself with the tree. "Does she know you feel that way?" She wondered what sort of things these two young ones talked about.

"No," he practically spit this word out. "I just wish her Mom liked me." And with that, he jumped down and ran to join the action around the Christmas tree.

Beth slowly released the breath she'd been holding.

Chapter Five

Daddy, wait. I forgot something." David popped his seatbelt and bolted out the car door. He raced inside, down the hall, and up the stairs. It was sitting on his desk—the model airplane he made from clay in art class a week ago. Mrs. Martin had been so impressed she offered to take it home and fire it in her kiln. She said this would help preserve it.

"Mom," he hollered, as he entered her study. "Quick, do you have a gift bag I can have? Dad's waiting for me."

She handed him a bag and some confetti from the closet. "You have fun with your grandfather and remember, behave."

Dashing out the door, he sighed, His mother was always telling him what to do as if he wouldn't remember. He climbed in the back seat. His father kept staring at him in the rear-view mirror as they drove to Grandfather Drake's office. "Is something wrong, Dad?"

"Uh…what? No, nothing's wrong." He parked in a huge garage. It was cold outside, but a fancy heated golf cart picked them up, taking them the rest of the way.

Excitement overcame David's nervousness. Grandfather Drake's office was close to the airport. He barely knew his grandfather, but he was super-excited to see planes being made and learn more about drones.

David gripped the gift bag by the handle and his other hand held his dad's as they got off the elevator and entered a huge office. One of the most beautiful Christmas trees David had ever seen sat in the center of the window, and "Rockin' around the Christmas Tree" played over the audio system.

A fancy lady, sitting behind a desk, greeted them. "Ah, you must be Mr. Drake's son and grandson."

"That's right," Phil acknowledged.

"Go on in. He's expecting you," she said.

Augustine Drake jumped up at the sight of them. "Phil, David, I've been waiting for you."

David set the bag on the coffee table while Phil shook hands. "Dad."

"Phil, you're my son. We should probably hug."

"Why? We never have before."

After an awkward moment, they finally came together in an uncoordinated hug.

The older man bent down to David's eye-level. "So, David, you've come to spend the day with your grandfather, have you?"

David walked without hesitation into the hug offered him.

"Son, I know you're probably swamped at the office," the senior Drake said. "You run along, now. I've cleared my schedule for the entire day. The boy will be fine with me."

Phil turned to his youngest. "David, are you going to be alright?"

David nodded.

After Phil left, his grandfather asked, "Do you want

to come and look at the various models of aircraft on the computer before we take a tour of the plant?"

"Of course." David stood beside him and watched the slideshow. Grandfather explained every model in chronological order: when it was designed, its mission, and whether it was still in commission. David oohed and aahed at the impressive designs, and not once did he get bored.

His grandfather became animated about certain designs, especially if they accomplished something the previous model did not. "Maybe you're a chip off your old grandfather's block, eh? Ever think you might like to build aerospace prototypes?"

"Proto…what? I think I know what you mean. It would be so cool. I really want to be a pilot, though, but my mom doesn't like that idea. She doesn't want me to crash." David rolled his eyes.

"Your mother may be wiser than we think. There are lots of other things you can do besides fly."

"Yeah, but I'm not sure yet. Maybe by the time I'm in sixth grade, I'll know what I want to do." David sat across from Mr. Drake at lunch and ate a corn dog with mac 'n' cheese. His grandfather gave him all of his attention.

"So, what is your favorite subject in school?"

He squinted and thought hard. "Math…no science. But I also like to read and write stories. I don't know. I like them all."

"Whoa. That's impressive."

David started to relax. His grandfather was kind of fun. "Can I ask you a question?"

"Yes, fire away."

"I heard you are sick. Are…are you going to die?"

Grandfather Drake cleared his throat. "Well, I suppose so. One day."

"Do you think you'll wish you'd done anything different?"

The old man hesitated and took a deep breath before answering. "I bet I will…" He stared at the floor and his voice trailed off, "I bet I will."

"Do you believe in God?" David scooped a heaping mouthful of mac 'n' cheese into his mouth.

His grandfather raised an eyebrow. "God?"

"Yes," David replied with his mouth half full. "because my mom and I pray for you each night before I go to bed."

The old man raised his head and stared at nothing across the room. His eyes became watery, but he blinked a lot, and they cleared. "Does your dad believe in God?"

"Of course. He's a wise man. 'Only a fool says in his heart there is no God.'"

Mr. Drake laughed, and David wasn't sure why. When they finished and were preparing to tour the plant, David remembered. "I forgot something in your office. Can we go get it?"

"Why sure. Do you need it now or can we get it later?"

"It's not for me."

When they reached the office, David picked up the bag and handed it to his grandfather. "Merry Christmas. Go on and open it." He leaned on the end of the sofa while his grandfather opened the gift. When he pulled out the bright blue model plane, David said, "I made it just for you, Grandpa."

"You made this for me?" His voice cracked.

"Yep, but my teacher fired it in something called a keln."

Grandfather Drake wrapped his arms around him. When David realized what he had said, he covered his mouth with his hand. "My dad and mom said I should call you Grandfather, but is it okay if I call you Grandpa? It's what I call my other grandpa."

The old man pulled out a handkerchief from his pocket and nodded.

Chapter Six

October 18, 2006

David sat at his and Aliyah's usual table in the noisy middle school lunchroom. Chad sat next to two of the football boys. Abby and Nicole sat down right after David.

"Where's Aliyah?" Chad asked. David was wondering the same thing.

Abby spoke up. "She was behind me in line. Probably be here in a minute."

Aliyah didn't arrive until ten minutes later, and she took her usual spot beside David. She had brought her lunch but perused the trays of their friends. "What are you guys eating today?"

While others answered, David asked, "Why did you bring your lunch?"

"They're leftovers." She smiled at him. He knew she often ate different things during a certain season. A minute later, she offered him a bag of cookies and a sealed homemade candied apple.

"What's this? Leftovers?"

"Yep." She bit into a cookie but continued talking.

"Cookies shaped like the Torah." She held one of his up. "Leftover from *Shemini Atzeret*."

"Shemin what?" asked Chad.

"It's one of her many Jewish holidays," David explained, "but I can't keep them all straight."

Aliyah punched his arm. "You have a lot of holidays, too, that I can't keep straight."

"Like what?"

"Christmas, Good Friday, Easter—" she rattled them off quickly until David interrupted.

"Yeah, but you know when they are. I never know when yours are. What are you observing now?"

"It's a joyous holiday, thus the cookies and apples. Kind of like your candy at Christmas. It's all about rejoicing in Adonai as His chosen people."

Twelve-year-old David stopped listening after Christmas. Instead, the animation of her face captured his attention. The color in her cheeks, the moist softness of her lips, the sway of her long black hair. She was his "chosen people" and he wanted to spend more time with her. Since starting middle school, they didn't get to ride the bus together most days because of football practice for him and other extracurricular activities. "What did your parents say about the dance this Saturday?" he asked.

She didn't answer right away. "Yeah, I can go, but I have to meet you there."

David sighed. "You didn't ask them, did you?"

"There's no point in me asking them. They'll just say no. This way we can still be together." She put her hand over his. "Trust me. I know my parents."

And he did trust her, but he also felt like they were doing something wrong. "Okay, I'll meet you there. But, what about your *bat mitzvah*? You're going to ask them to invite me, right?"

Her lips parted as if she were going to say something else, but then she nodded. "Of course." The bell rang, signifying five minutes until their fourth-period class, one they did not share.

David felt grumpy the rest of the afternoon. Even in sixth-period science, a time they shared, he refused to write Aliyah notes on the notebook they used to communicate during class.

Sitting in the desk beside him, she grabbed it and jotted down, *I said I'm going to ask them, Dave.*

He crossed out *Dave* and wrote *DAVID* in all caps.

She grabbed it out of his hands, smiling. *Let me know what color shirt you're wearing to the dance, and I'll try to match it, DAVID.*

~

That Saturday, David showered and used cologne Melissa had given him last year for Christmas. He and Aliyah had sampled it at the mall, and she liked it, so he'd put it on his Christmas wish list. He buttoned his magenta shirt and tied his teal green tie, smiling at his image in the mirror. It didn't look too good on him, but magenta was his favorite color on Aliyah. It highlighted her skin tone and brought out the color in her face.

He watched her walk into the gymnasium. Her high-waisted, below-the-knee magenta dress swayed with each step and she wore her long hair down, flowing freely. She smiled as he approached.

Then as if she'd forgotten something, she opened her purse and frantically searched. With a grin, she retrieved a teal green clip. Aliyah pulled up portions of her hair on either side and fastened them in the back with the clip.

Then she did a three-sixty. They matched, but more importantly, she was beautiful.

"Nice."

"You like that? I found it in my mom's things, so I 'borrowed' it."

David took her hand and led her to the punch bowl.

~

The sound of Justin Timberlake singing "My Love" played as lights flickered from the disco ball hanging in the middle of the dimly lit gymnasium. It felt natural when David took Aliyah's hand. After all, they were friends. He was her best friend. Aliyah looked at the other girls. They were all dressed quite fashionably but not her. She was lucky her parents had let her wear this. But David didn't seem to mind. He always made her feel comfortable, maybe even special. She couldn't explain it.

"You smell nice," she told him. He was wearing the cologne she loved.

Chad and Abby joined them, giggling about something. "Hey, 'Liyah." Abby said while dipping punch.

"The two of you match." Chad observed.

David stared at him and then pushed him.

Chad objected. "What? It's true."

Aliyah compared the two of them. Chad was wearing a polo shirt over a polo shirt. They were contrasting colors of green and the sleeves on the one underneath were a bit longer. "Let me guess, Chad." Aliyah smiled slyly. "You couldn't figure out which shirt to wear so you wore them both."

The three of them laughed, but Chad protested, tugging at his collars. "Hey, I'm rockin' the Timberlake look."

"Yeah," David piped in. "It's some look." He stood about three inches taller than Chad. His dark brown hair and blue eyes set him apart, Aliyah thought. Chad was skinny with a big nose. David was perfect and the best friend anyone could ask for. Most girls had a best girlfriend, but not her. True, she'd invited Abby over to her house a few times, but ever since the second grade, it had been David and her.

David played quarterback for the middle school football team, and Aliyah often tried to spend Thursday evenings at Abby's so she could watch David play. She would watch him throw the ball and sometimes run with it, and she struggled to understand the game.

When the music started playing "Chasing Cars," Chad and Abby disappeared.

Aliyah raised her eyebrows and grinned. "Come on, let's dance."

It was a slow song, and as she danced in his arms, she didn't feel the least bit uncomfortable. The lyrics became forever tied to her feelings for David; two people lying beside each other and forgetting the world. She wished she could forget the world—her world—one of which he was forbidden to be a part. Aliyah hoped he wouldn't bring up her bat mitzvah tonight. How was she going to tell him her parents would never invite him? No, she would be expected to meet and even dance with acceptable Jewish boys at her 'coming-of-age' celebration, which was only one week away.

Halfway through the song, David stared into her eyes. Aliyah forgot all about next week, forgot all about respectable Jewish boys. All that mattered was this moment and everything their eyes were saying that their lips could not. She didn't want the song to end, but it did, and so did the night.

Soon she was in the car; her parents up front talking about the plans for next week and her in the back seat, dreaming of David.

"Aliyah, tomorrow we're going to pick up your dress in Hartford, and your father's going to finalize the hall."

She nodded and stared out the window.

~

It was finally Wednesday, Aliyah's twelfth birthday. David was seated in his usual spot on the bus behind Melissa.

She turned around and crossed her fingers. "Good luck, little brother."

He nodded. Melissa understood how important this was to him. A wrapped present sat on the seat beside David awaiting Aliyah's stop. Today, she would let him know what her parents decided about his attendance on Saturday. Surely, they could see he was a good guy.

The bus brakes squealed as it came to a stop and Aliyah climbed aboard. His eyes met hers as she walked down the aisle. She didn't smile, already eradicating his hopes. He picked up the present in haste to make room for her to sit. When she saw it, she grinned.

"What's that?"

"It's your birthday present."

She reached for it, but he held it away from her, shaking his head. "Huh-uh. You first. What did they say?"

She stretched across in a scuffle to reach it and fell on him, their mouths coming within an inch of each other. Hers smelled like peppermint. He couldn't resist. In a split second, he closed the distance and gave her an innocent peck on the lips.

Aliyah looked startled. For that matter, so was he. A rush of feelings flooded his body. When her eyes twinkled and her mouth curved up, he wanted more but controlled himself. Clearing his throat, he surrendered the gift to her.

She fell back in the seat and started ripping the paper off. He held his breath. When she opened the box to find the ring, an opal birthstone set in white gold with three diamonds on either side, a tear slipped down her cheek.

"You don't like it?" He couldn't conceal his disappointment.

She shook her head. "I love it. I've always wanted one and you found it, exactly the way I'd told you."

"Then, what's wrong?"

More tears spilled before she wiped them away. She stared at the ring. Then, she closed the box and handed it back to him. "I can't keep it."

"But why not?" The bus was approaching the school.

She took his hand in hers. "This Shabbat is the celebration of me becoming a young woman. There will be dancing and a celebration." With a downcast look, she shook her head and her hair fell to the front of her shoulders. "My parents won't allow you to come or to spend any time with me…ever. After a few years, I'll marry 'a nice Jewish boy.' That's what's expected."

It was as if she had punched him in the stomach. He had no words. One by one, all the kids filed out of the bus, leaving only them.

"David, we should go," she said softly.

He arose and stepped back, moving his arm in a wide swing. "You go ahead. I'll get my things together."

~

Aliyah couldn't stop the tears, so she ran for the nearest restroom. In the privacy of the stall her tears flowed freely.

"'Liyah, is that you?" Abby asked.

Aliyah scrunched up her face, wishing she hadn't been discovered. "Yeah."

"What's up, girl?"

Aliyah quickly wiped away the evidence and put on a good face before unlocking the door. She crossed to the sink and washed her hands. "Oh, nothing. I'm fine, really."

"Did David say something?"

She cocked her head to the side. "No. It's not David." Drying her hands on a paper towel, Aliyah confided the awful happenings of last night. "When I told my parents that David wanted to come to my bat mitzvah, they freaked. You would have thought I'd committed a treasonous act worthy of death. Mom started swearing and Dad said he was going to put in for a transfer at work."

"Oh, 'Liyah, that's awful. You don't think he will, do you?"

"I'm not sure of anything right now." She grabbed her bag and headed to the door. "We'd better get to class."

October 28th, 2006

This momentous occasion excited everyone inside the festively decorated pavilion in Hartford, all except Aliyah who couldn't shake the week's exchanges with David. After the family had been introduced, Aliyah, dressed in white linen with flowers adorning her hair, lit the candles and her father recited the *Hamotzi* before the *kiddush* cup and *challah* bread were passed around to be shared.

The invisible spotlight shone on Aliyah as family and friends honored their God and her. She put on a brave face, one that hopefully concealed her sadness. Never in a million years would she have chosen to hurt her best friend.

Soon the music played. She danced with her father and then came the *horah*, where everyone danced in a circle. Then, they pulled up a chair, pushed her into it, and hoisted her up in the air. She gasped, her stomach flipped, and her smile was genuine but short-lived.

As the day progressed, Aliyah opened gifts—savings bonds, money, and *Judaica*, but none compared to the opal ring she had to refuse. She danced with Caleb, Joshua, and Aaron—everyone except the one she truly longed to be with. She danced until her feet hurt and the torturous day eventually ended.

Aliyah hoped her parents couldn't see her true emotions. She hoped her fake expressions of joy and excitement concealed the truth; a hope that evaporated that evening when she climbed into bed and could hear her parents arguing in their bedroom next to hers.

"We should never have moved here," her mother, Esther, yelled. "It's you who will have to answer for this." Drawers slammed and Aliyah flinched.

"You're her mother. Couldn't you have taught her to respect her elders and make sure she knew what Adonai expected from her?"

"Hmph. If we'd never moved here, we wouldn't be arguing about this now."

"Enough," her father, Yosef, yelled. "I'm going to

accept the position in Tel Aviv. We'll move at the end of the year. Until then, she's not to see that boy or talk to him on the phone. Nothing. Do you hear me?"

Aliyah couldn't hear her mother's answer. All fell silent. She buried her face in her pillow and sobbed quietly.

~

David couldn't stop thinking about Aliyah. How was her day? What happened at her bat mitzvah? Did she dance with boys? Of course, she did. All these years, she'd known all along that she couldn't like him. It didn't seem to matter to her that they couldn't have a future. If he had known, he would have guarded his heart. Still, he just wanted the phone to ring and to hear her voice. He finally fell asleep and the next morning, his family went to church. Surely, she'd call him sometime this afternoon.

No call came.

When Aliyah boarded the bus Monday morning, David didn't remember her ever looking so dreadful. He watched her every step of the way to the back of the bus where they'd been sitting since before middle school. Darkness encircled her eyes and an aura of gloom surrounded her solemn face. When she sat down, he decided against complaining about her lack of calling.

"Is it that bad?" he ventured.

"It's worse." Tears threatened to spill over her eyelids.

He waited for her to compose herself, but when she couldn't, he asked, "What happened?"

"Oh, David." The tears overflowed. "I'm not allowed to talk to you."

He raised his voice. "What?" Her ridiculous parents

were being unreasonable.

"And…we're moving…to Tel Aviv." She sobbed, and he took her in his arms, letting her cry into his shoulder. It took a moment for the weight of her announcement to register. When it did, he panicked. How would he live without her?

The next few days, they used their notebook more than ever. They filled page after page. They ate lunches together, they laughed and refused to think about the day Aliyah would travel with her family to the other side of the world, leaving them both heartbroken.

Chapter Seven

Without consulting David and Aliyah, Hanukkah came and went, not much different than it had in the past. Right after it came the last day of school before Christmas break. Their goodbyes had been in progress since before Thanksgiving.

As the bus followed the curvy road, David pleaded, "Why can't you email me?"

"Because my dad will know and be furious. I can't disobey him like that."

"I don't want you to, either, but we have to find a way to communicate." He brushed her hair away from her face. "I'm going to miss you."

She lifted her eyes from the dirty bus floor and gazed into his. "I'll write when I get the chance."

"Send me your telephone number as soon as you can. I'll have Melissa call, and then after you get on the line, she'll give the phone to me." It sounded like a good plan in his head.

"Okay." She started crying. "I don't want to go."

He wrapped his arms around her, and they embraced. David wanted to hang on and never let go. Sitting in the back of the bus, none of the other students bothered them as they held onto each other.

She whispered in his ear, "I'll miss you so much. You're my best friend."

At that, he pulled away, searching her eyes. "Aliyah…you're more than my best friend." He wiped her tears away and lifted her chin. With all the courage he could summon, he proclaimed what he had known since the second grade. "I love you. I always have."

Her eyes brightened and her face beamed. "I love you, too." She cocked her head sideways and grinned, "Dave."

He laughed but didn't correct her. She could call him anything. David kissed her lightly, but let his lips linger. Hers were soft and sweet and perfect. He would never have come up for air if the brakes of the bus hadn't squealed as it came to a halt in front of her house. She walked away from the bus, her long curly hair swaying in the wind. She turned and waved goodbye, an image he'd never forget.

~

Christmas came and went. New Year's, too. Still no word from Aliyah. David felt himself drowning in a sea of emotions, ones he couldn't control. He longed to see her face, hear her voice, kiss like they had over and over again, and nothing made the ache go away. He would always remember that night of the school dance and how pretty she looked. David had framed the night's picture of the two of them and placed it on his desk. He cherished the memory of their first kiss when she refused the opal ring and their last one that fateful day on the bus before the holidays.

Alone in his room, David opened the notebook, the

one in which he and Aliyah wrote notes back and forth at school. He lost himself in her handwriting and imagined her being there with him. He smiled at pages where she'd written Dave and he had crossed it out and wrote DAVID. This book would become his most read book ever. He spent hours in it, laughing, crying, dreaming. It was all he had left of her.

Aliyah never called. She never wrote letters, and she never emailed. After two years David placed the book in a box, along with the framed picture that had sat on his desk, the remaining cologne in his bottle, and other memorabilia—anything that reminded him of her. He spent some time reflecting on his soul mate, sort of like a funeral. Then, he put the box on the highest shelf of his closet and closed the door.

~

One year later

Melissa answered her phone.

"Um, is this Mel?" The voice was deep and low.

Why is Hunter Williams, the handsome senior in my sociology class, calling me? He was popular and taller than most with blond hair and a touch of whiskers peppering his face into a sophisticated shadow.

"Yes…Hunter?"

"Uh-huh. Did you complete the homework assignment for tomorrow?"

"Yes, but—"

"You know—" There was a pause and he cleared his throat. "That's not the reason I called. I was wondering if you'd like to go to dinner and a movie Saturday night?"

She could have squealed but kept it inside. Her mind

raced to come up with an acceptable answer. "Sure, but I have to see if my parents have any other plans first. Can I call you back?" That gave her an escape without looking juvenile if her parents said no. Up until this point, she'd only group dated, but car dating was allowed when she had turned sixteen. She just hadn't been asked. *Quick, I have to think of something else to say so he continues talking.* "What movie did you have in mind?"

"We could see *The Babysitters* or *The Tracy Fragments*. It doesn't matter to me."

Both of those movies were rated R. She wasn't allowed to see those, so she needed to come up with another choice. She remembered David saying something about *Iron Man 2*, and many of the kids at school were going. At least, it wouldn't sound like an immature suggestion. "What about *Iron Man*? I'd like to see it, would you?"

"Yeah, that's fine. It doesn't matter to me."

"I'll talk to my mom and see if I'm free. Then I'll call you back."

As soon as she hung up the phone, she blasted out of her room, squealing. She ran down the stairs. "Mom, Dad? Where are you guys?"

"I'm in the kitchen," Beth answered.

Melissa leaned against the island and stopped to catch her breath. "Guess who just asked me out?"

She had her mom's full attention now, who stopped chopping vegetables and studied her. "Who?"

"Hunter Williams. That's who."

"Isn't that Stacy Williams' son?"

Melissa's mouth dropped. "I suppose so. Who cares who his mom is? I'm not dating his mom. He's like the most popular boy in our school." She started jumping up and down. "—and he asked me out," she shrieked.

Phil and David had just come into the house from the garage prior to her announcement.

"Only the two of you?" her father asked.

The smile left her face. This might not be good. There could be resistance. "It's a date, Dad. You know, the boy picks you up in his car and you go to dinner and a movie?" Her mom and dad exchanged looks.

"Hunter Williams?" David raised his eyebrows and shook his head.

"Do you know him, David?" her mother asked.

"Not personally, but I know who he is."

"Oh, come on," Melissa protested. "He doesn't know anything. I thought I could car date after I turned sixteen."

Again, her parents exchanged looks, but it was her dad who laid down the requirements. "We'll want to know the actual name of his parents, their address, telephone number, and his cell phone if he has one. And you'll have to be home by eleven o'clock. We have church the next morning."

"Midnight, Dad, please? Most movies start around nine and end a little after eleven. I'll be ready for church the next morning. I promise."

Phil took a deep breath. "Okay, but not one minute later. And he has to come inside and meet us first."

Melissa exhaled as if deflated. "Oh, come on, dad. Nobody does that anymore. Besides, you can be so intimidating."

Her dad raised one eyebrow. "That's the idea." He headed to the bathroom to wash his hands, and Melissa knew it wasn't up for discussion. She glared at David.

He hadn't helped the situation any.

"What?" David shrugged. "I didn't say anything."

Her mom finished the topic. "Melissa, you heard your father. He only has your best interest at heart."

Melissa stormed off but not without adding, "This family is impossible."

~

Phil and Beth watched TV in the den Saturday night past their normal bedtime. Each kept checking their watch as the minutes passed by. Phil finally started pacing. "This is awful," he announced. "Teenagers should not date. We need to rethink the rules."

Beth agreed. "Should we call her?" she asked.

"Yes," Phil answered. "But first, where's Hunter's and his parent's phone numbers? If his parents aren't awake, perhaps they should be."

When Beth rose to get them, the phone rang. She rushed to it. "Hello." She held the phone where Phil could hear crying followed by sniffling.

"Mom?"

Melissa's voice sounded weak, making the hair on his neck stand up.

Beth sought answers. "Melissa? Where are you? What's wrong?"

Phil clenched his teeth, and his hands balled up into fists at his side.

"No, Mom, I'm fine. Can you come pick me up?"

"Sure, honey. Where are you?"

"I'm walking on Highway 7 just south of Pop's Diner."

Beth gasped. "I'm on my way."

"I'm going, too," Phil announced when she hung up.

"Yes, I know," Beth answered as they walked out the

door.

It was about a ten-minute drive to the spot Melissa described, but Phil made it there in six. Melissa was walking in the dark on the side of the road with no sign of Hunter. His blood boiled. Phil pounded his fist on the steering wheel.

"Phil, calm down," Beth told him as he swung the car around. She jumped out and wrapped her arms around their daughter.

Melissa climbed in the back seat and closed the door. Her eyes were swollen and her face splotchy from crying, signs Phil recognized from fourteen years of fathering her. He steered the car back onto the highway and said, "I'll kill him. I swear, I'll kill him."

"No, Dad, please—"

"Tell me what happened. What did he do?"

Beth placed her hand on Phil's arm, "Dear, please."

"He didn't do anything," Melissa cried. "Not that he didn't want to. After the movie, he drove out into the country, even though I objected."

Phil clenched his jaw again as the dash lights illuminated his face.

"He kissed me…it was gross…and then he…I struggled and broke free. I jumped out of the car and started walking."

Phil slammed on the brakes and turned all the way around. "Honey, did he—"

Melissa stared at him and then her eyes widened. "NO! I stopped him. When I started walking, he said he'd drive me home, but I refused to get back in the car."

Beth reached over the seat and grasped her hand. "You did the right thing, honey. Although I'd have called us sooner rather than later."

"He stopped as he passed me and hollered out the window, 'grow up, sophomore.'" She sniffed. "Then he peeled out and left me in complete darkness."

"I'll kill him," Phil said under his breath. "I'll still kill him."

After they returned home, and Melissa had been settled in her bed, Phil and Beth retired to their bedroom. "Let me rephrase it. I won't 'kill him,' but he'll wish he were dead when I get through with him."

Beth crawled beneath the sheets. "Phil, 'vengeance is mine, saith the Lord,'" she reminded him. "You're supposed to love your enemies. That young man needs our prayers that God will help him see the error in his ways."

Phil sighed. Sometimes his faith required more of him than he believed possible.

Chapter Eight

August 2012

The summer sun rose over the pond as the ducks bathed in the water and bluebirds flitted from tree to tree. Beth loved her early mornings, sitting by the pool and reading her devotional. In years past, it was her quiet time before the chaotic morning began with the kids preparing for school or other activities.

After today, life would never be the same. She closed her book and walked back to the house along the path beside the fragrant rose bushes. As she entered through the side, a tear spilled down her cheek when she noticed the mudroom doorframe with its etched markings, recording the heights of the children as they had grown over the years. She reached up and ran her fingers over the latest one of David's, six foot-one-inch height. Barely passing his dad, he stood above them all.

Losing Melissa, who had been attending Harvard the last two years, had been hard enough, but when David graduated last spring, the empty-nest syndrome became a stark reality. In just a few short hours, David and his girlfriend, Shelby, would be leaving for Ithaca, New

York. Beth had wanted Phil and her to be the ones to help David get settled on campus, but strong-willed, independent David insisted he and Shelby would go alone.

Phil had been mentioning trips the two of them could take and other advantages of being middle-aged, but she couldn't embrace that yet. He seemed to recognize she was struggling with her emotions, but Beth believed that if *he* struggled at all, he was doing a good job of concealing it.

Phil had mentioned renewing their vows and taking the honeymoon they never had. Since their marriage in September of 1993, they always had children. At that time Melissa was twenty months old and David was born nine months later. Beth supposed renewing their vows and honeymooning in Italy could be fun.

They had been to Europe once with the kids, Hawaii, and multiple trips to Disney World. Other than that, they usually went once a year with a mission group to Africa. She and Melissa went with the ladies teaching women and children, while Phil and David worked with a team digging wells and teaching village leaders good sanitation practices.

Beth had just poured a cup of coffee when Phil entered the kitchen and smiled at her. She handed him a cup, but he set it down on the island.

He took her in his arms and held her tight. "It's going to be alright. We'll get through this together."

Beth always found comfort and strength in his embrace. She stared into his eyes and smiled. "I know." Then her lips met his in a kiss that said everything they weren't voicing. *I love you; I'll always be here; you are my everything.*

~

The early morning sun streaked through the blinds of David's bedroom. He pressed his phone next to his ear with his shoulder while continuing to pack. His room looked like a disaster area. He sighed in irritation. "Shelby, I told you. We can put it in the back of the truck." He was referring to the vanity she kept complaining about not being able to move. "How many boxes do you have?" This he asked while trying to hold the phone and pull his duffle bag off the top shelf of his closet.

"I have four medium and one large," she answered.

He heard Shelby's answer, but the phone slipped and fell to the floor. David abandoned his reach and turned to retrieve it. A box fell to the floor behind him.

"You still there?" he asked her.

"Yes, I'm here."

"How large is the big one?" He stepped over a pile on the floor and looked to see what fell.

It was a black box—one he remembered well. The lid had come off and its contents lay sprawled around it. A picture of a younger him and a girl in a magenta dress stared up at him. Shelby was rattling on about something, but he came to a complete halt and slid to the floor.

"—and the comforter. I have a box with my makeup, mirrors, flat irons, and curling irons. It took one whole box just for my shoes and—"

"Shelby, I gotta go. I'll call you back later."

"uh…, we're still leaving by noon, right?"

He didn't answer before hanging up. He couldn't listen to her fuss and fret over nothing anymore.

Slowly, David took the box and started picking up the pieces one by one. He placed the ticket stubs from

Superman Returns and *The Notebook* back inside, movies he and Aliyah saw together only because her parents believed she was going with Abby. They stole every moment they could, and perhaps that was wrong. He sprayed some of the cologne on, True Star by Tommy Hilfiger, and memories rushed in like the torrential waves of a tsunami. He conjured up an image of her glowing face and her laughter echoed in his mind. Pain stabbed his heart. All through high school, he kept telling himself it was just puppy love. It couldn't have meant anything, but it did. No one could convince him otherwise.

David opened the CD case and slipped the disk in his player. Snow Patrol's "Chasing Cars" filled the room with melodic memories. Leaning back against the wall, he listened to the familiar words about two people lying beside each other and forgetting the world. The disk was set to repeat, and when it started over again, he climbed onto the bed, and stared at the ceiling before closing his eyes and losing himself in the past. Memories of their cheeks pressing together as they danced to this song. His fists tightened and his jaw clenched. No, he would not cry.

David rolled over and retrieved the black spiral notebook from the box. He opened it and read his printed scribble: *November 7, 2001. Do you like to play video games?*

Her reply: *Yes, but I don't have any.*

Several exclamation points were his response.

Do you? What games do you have?

I just got Tetris. I could bring it with me. We could play on the bus.

He remembered her toothless smile, and he chuckled

to himself as he recollected bringing Tetris and watching her body mimicking her play moves. He turned several pages. December 15th, 2006. *My dad says we're leaving the day after Christmas break. Can you meet me at the mall this weekend, Dave?*

He'd crossed out Dave and wrote DAVID. *Sure, what time? But will your parents let you? They haven't let you do anything since your bat mitzvah.*

If I tell them I'm meeting Abby, they might let me come. That rendezvous never happened. Hard as they tried to find time together, her parents blocked every attempt during their last months before she left his world.

He jumped as his mother spoke from the door. "You're not going to be ready if you're just lying around."

"I'm not lying around, mom." He stood and tossed the book in the box. Then he picked up a pair of shoes and chunked them with such force into a box of packing his mom flinched, and he immediately regretted it.

"David, Are you alright? Is there anything I can help with?"

"No!" With deliberate heavy steps, he crossed to the door. "Just let me do my own thing." His temper flared, angry at a world that denied him what he wanted. Frustrated that he had no control over his fate with Aliyah, he slammed the door shut in front of his mother, something he'd never done before. David sighed and ran his fingers through his hair. He took a deep breath and opened the door again.

She stopped a few steps down the hall and turned around.

"Mom, I'm sorry. I didn't mean that."

"It's okay." She pursed her lips, returned, and

hugged him.

He knew she was trying not to cry. "I love you, mom."

"I know, son. It's just that I'm going to miss you." She grabbed him again.

He knew a storm raged inside him, but his mom was going through a difficult time too. Still, why was she so emotional about him leaving?

After she walked away, he threw the last of the contents inside the black box. He picked up the blue case with the opal ring without opening it and tossed it in the box. Then he kicked the box under his bed, out of sight. Maybe later he'd throw it all away, but not now.

David's cell phone rang. From the annoying ringtone he'd assigned to Shelby, he knew who it was. He touched the ignore button.

Sometimes a little bit of Shelby went a long way. They had started dating their senior year. She was a cheerleader, a real knockout, and she knew it. Shelby spent way too much time on her blond hair cutting, lengthening, straightening, and curling it. Her long lashes curved above blue eyes, and white teeth gleamed in a perfect row, made possible by her orthodontist. Her family attended the same church as his, and somehow this was important to him.

When he said he was applying to Cornell, Shelby told him she thought it was one that offered cheer scholarships. When his application was accepted, she announced that she had received a scholarship and would be joining him. Shelby even suggested they travel together on moving day. Each of them was staying in the dorms so it made sense to him. That way David didn't have to tell his parents goodbye on campus in front of the other students.

~

It took almost five hours before David and Shelby exited at Mitchell Street in Ithaca. As they turned onto College Avenue, students milled about the shops and eateries. This was it, what he had worked for.

Shelby squealed at the Starbuck's on the corner. "That's it, David. That's where we'll spend most of our time, studying and drinking coffee."

David couldn't help but smile. Her eyes sparkled with excitement. He put his arm around her and pulled her closer, if that were possible. She always sat next to him with their thighs touching.

"You think so, huh? What about the library?"

"Nope. That's way too boring. At least at Starbucks, we can run into other students."

"Shel, I don't think I'm going to have much of a social life, not if I'm going to pursue law or business."

"David, hello? This is college. We only do it once. This is our chance to live it up without parents and rules."

He turned the corner and parked in front of Balch Hall. She bounced out of the truck and waved at a girl, who ran to meet her, the two of them hugging and giggling.

It was just as well. He wouldn't have pursued the conversation further anyway. He knew what he was doing here, and that was what mattered. David released the tailgate as Shelby dragged the girl to the truck. "Chelsea, this is my boyfriend, David."

Chelsea's cunning smile and twinkling eye indicated her approval of him, and he shrugged off her demure greeting before reaching for the closest box.

"Here, let me help you with that." A strapping young

man in shorts and a Philadelphia Eagles T-shirt was reaching for the next box.

"David," Chelsea spoke, "This is my boyfriend, Sam."

"Hey, Sam. Eagles, huh?"

Sam acknowledged David's Giants shirt. "Yeah, always looking for a good debate."

"Wearing that shirt around here may get you more than a 'debate.'" David returned with a laugh.

With Sam's help, the two of them swiftly delivered the vanity up to Shelby's dorm.

"Hey, Chels, maybe they'd like to get some pizza with us later," Sam suggested.

Chelsea added, "Yeah, Shelby. There's a pizza place we found on the corner about three or four blocks away."

Shelby looked at David. He nodded. "Sounds good. Give me a bit of time to unload and get settled. Is eight o'clock okay?"

"Sure. You need any help?" Sam offered.

"No, I got it. She brought the most."

David kissed Shelby before climbing in the truck and driving across campus to his dorm. That's when it hit him. He was actually here. An adult, not living at home anymore. Passing by McGraw Hall and Sage Hall, he remembered one of the reasons this campus appealed to him. Its gothic style in the older buildings reminded him of Harry Potter's world. Lofty, centuries-old oak and elm trees provided ample shade throughout the campus.

~

The phone rang and Beth slammed the book closed she'd been reading in the study and rushed to answer it. She'd been waiting almost seven hours for David to call and let them know he'd arrived without mishap. Her mind jumped to all sorts of conclusions.

"Hello." Beth expected to hear his familiar voice, but instead, there was silence.

"Hello?" She repeated.

"Um," it was a young female voice she didn't recognize. "Is this the Drake residence?"

Oh, please, Lord, no. Don't let this be some stranger calling to tell me my son's been hurt or worse! "Yes, it is." Beth held her breath.

"Um…may I talk to David, please?"

"He's not here." Beth sighed with relief. "May I tell him who called?"

"Uh…I'll just call him later."

Before Beth could tell this unknown young lady that he had left for college, the phone clicked. She'd hung up. Beth stared at the receiver.

She had allowed David ample time to do the adult thing and call home. She dialed his number and waited for her son to answer.

Chapter Nine

The sun shone bright and the warmth of August was welcomed on campus. Soon the temperatures would drop, leaves would fall, and green grass would turn brown. Students gathered on the lawn in front of the financial affairs office, chatting and laughing at a shared joke, some looking at their cell phones, others taking selfies. Girls wore low-cut jeans with intentional holes in them, some with short t-shirts, exposing their skin and belly button piercings. In the distance near one of the residence halls, some guys threw a football around.

As usual, Aliyah could feel everyone staring at her as she walked out of the office and down the sidewalk. She had been in the states for only two days now, just enough time to get settled into her dorm and meet her roommate, but not enough time to go shopping—definitely not enough time to make new friends. Her long gray skirt fell beneath her knees. Luckily, her white shirt had short sleeves in this heat. Her ankle socks barely showed above her boxy athletic shoes. These sneakers were her mother's best suggestion because walking all over this campus required comfortable shoes.

Aliyah had just confirmed that all of her papers were in order—the scholarships she'd earned, and her financial aid. Now, she needed to go to admissions and see about changing the government class for which she hadn't signed up but found herself enrolled in.

She headed across the grass, up the steps, and through the door. As she waited in line, Aliyah noted the crest above the clock on the wall. *Cornell University Founded AD 1865*. It felt strange to be back on U.S. soil, but she was thankful she'd finally talked her parents into letting her come. Of course, it was under the condition that she would keep close contact with her aunt and uncle in New York. At least she wouldn't have to worry about marrying Jacob Steiner for another four years. He was getting his education in Tel Aviv and, with any luck, would fall in love with a nice Jewish girl, releasing her from her fate forever. She wasn't going to worry about that. For now, she'd savor every day of freedom she could. One day at a time.

~

David sighed and shifted from one foot to the other while waiting in line to change one of his classes. A lot of arguing came from the counter and, although he couldn't hear, from the clerk's squinted eyes and her stern look, he guessed the girl in the long gray skirt was losing the battle. Her long wavy black hair extended to her thighs. How difficult it must be to brush. Every once in a while, she'd fling black strands to the back with her hand. Her attire did nothing for her slender form. She was probably an inch or so taller than Shelby, the girl he compared all others to.

His phone slipped out of its case and fell to the floor. When he bent to retrieve it, he noticed a text from

Shelby: *Hey Sexy. Want to come and take me to Starbucks? I need a latte.* It chimed and another text popped up. *Where are you? Why are you ignoring me?*

David rolled his eyes and glanced ahead to see if the line had moved. The girl had vanished, and the people ahead advanced a few steps. Where did she go? David couldn't help himself. He checked the whole room. No sign of her. Wonder what her face looked like. She might have been a Quaker, but if so, she'd wear a head covering. He peered at the plaque on the wall. "*I would found an institution where any person can find instruction in any study.*" *Ezra Cornell.* His eyes drifted down to the window. That's when he saw the girl with long black hair, walking away. He couldn't take his eyes off her. She stopped, dropped her bag to the ground, and raked her hair back, fastening it with a clip.

There was something familiar about her, though she was a good distance away. She reminded him of an older Aliyah. Surely, he'd only imagined the teal color of the clip in her hair because he couldn't possibly see that far. Still, he abandoned his place and rushed outside and down the steps. By the time he rounded the corner, she'd disappeared. He ran hard in that direction, searching as he ran, but it was no use. He saw no signs of her. *This is silly. Aliyah is in Tel Aviv halfway around the globe. But, what if…*

The phone in his pocket sounded Shelby's annoying ringtone. He sighed and answered.

"Where are you?" Shelby sounded agitated. "I've been trying to contact you all morning."

"I've been waiting in line at the admissions office."

"Well, are you through? Can you take me to Starbucks?"

He ran his hands through his hair. "Yeah, I'll be there in ten."

~

After the dismissal of Aliyah's last class at two o'clock, she hurried to the dorm to drop off her books. She couldn't wait to go shopping for some different clothes. She was tired of the drab, modest attire required at her previous school. The sun beat down, and a gentle breeze caressed her face. She closed her eyes momentarily and enjoyed being free. Aliyah missed her little sister, but it would take more time to start missing her mom and dad. She strolled toward downtown and decided to walk past the Center for Jewish living. She owed a lot to that center. If it wasn't for it, her parents might not have let her come at all. Not forgetting her task at hand, she continued onto Seneca Street and picked up her pace.

By the time she returned, she sported a tight pair of jeans, a red Cornell t-shirt, and carried several bags. With new earbuds in her ears, she listened to her favorite playlist: "Roar" by Katy Perry, "As Long as You Love Me" by Justin Bieber, and all her favorites. She couldn't remember feeling this excited in a long time. Inhaling a deep breath, she smiled.

Then a song she had not anticipated shuffled in—"Chasing Cars" by Snow Patrol—she eyed an empty bench ahead and decided to sit for a while. The lyrics sounded in her ears, and she closed her eyes. Memories flowed of David at the middle school dance, so handsome in his khakis and magenta shirt. That teal green tie stood out against the magenta like a Christmas tree in a synagogue, but it was their thing, the colors that paired the two of them, if only for a night. His dark hair and blue eyes; their cheeks touching, both of them only twelve-years-old. They hadn't needed anyone just like the song said. They forgot it all and chased cars if only for a season in time.

Aliyah had tried to call David when she arrived. Her heart pounded and her palms sweated, but she wanted to talk to him, wanted to explain why she hadn't contacted him all those years. But it was foolish to call. To dredge up feelings that needed to be buried. She was glad he wasn't home that day. Reconnecting with him would either break her heart or break his. No, she'd enjoy her college years and then do what was expected of her. But no matter what, her resolve couldn't erase the memories. Those were hers to keep forever.

~

It was Tuesday and David's first day in his government class. He arrived early and took a seat toward the top in the auditorium-style seating. It was the first chance he'd had to open his book and take a look at it. He scanned through the table of contents as students started filing in. An older gentleman in a gray suit walked in and set his attaché on the desk.

"Good Morning, students. I'm professor Hartman. If you're to attend my class, you'll have to be on time and in your seats. No interruptions are allowed." At that moment, the door creaked open.

David looked at the blond beauty who walked in. *Wait a minute…that's Shelby*!

"You're late," Professor Hartman snapped.

"Sorry," she managed before searching the room. She spotted David and began climbing the stairs, her shoes clunking with every step.

Hartman arched his eyebrows and cleared his throat

before turning and writing the class requirements and grading components on the whiteboard.

Shelby sat in the seat beside David. “What’s his problem?” she whispered.

Hartman continued talking. “Now, let’s just see how much you know. What are some different types of governing?”

One student offered, “There’s dictatorship.”

“Democracy,” offered another.

“Yes.” He wrote down each answer before addressing the students again. “And someone else?” The room remained silent. Hartman lifted his gaze. “Miss Late, any suggestions?”

David wished he’d spoken up before. It might have spared Shelby the embarrassment of everyone staring at her.

She stuttered, “Uh…” Her face reddened.

He felt for her. Then a movement in his peripheral vision caught his eye. A raised hand from one of the front rows. It diverted everyone’s attention. He placed a comforting hand on Shelby’s.

“Yes?” Hartman asked.

“There are monarchies.” A female voice answered.

David’s ears perked up and his head jerked forward. That voice…so familiar. He searched the area of the hand, but all he saw were rows of heads. His heart pounded and the hair on his arms raised. He saw this one girl with long black hair, thick and wavy. She almost reminded him of the girl he saw at admissions, but it probably wasn’t her.

David stared at her the rest of class. He heard nothing. Instead, his thoughts were far removed. *What is wrong with me? Maybe it’s because that box dropped from my shelf in the closet and stirred up the past. Maybe any girl with long black hair reminds me of Aliyah.*

When Hartman dismissed them, David tried to see past the students walking in front of him, but by the time the crowd cleared, the girl was gone. He made his way down the stairs with Shelby's shoes clunking beside him.

She broke his trance. "Want to grab some lunch?"

He nodded and forced himself to be attentive. "What sounds good?" He asked, knowing they had several choices here on campus. They walked out the door and into the hall.

"Want some burgers and fries?" Shelby grabbed his wrist "We could go to Trillium. It's close." She checked her watch before rejoining his side.

David stopped. Mere feet in front of him, a girl stood staring out the window. He forgot about lunch and Shelby. The girl set her bag on the table, pulled out a clip, and fastened part of her long black hair in it. Teal green! Was she…is she Aliyah? Could that possibly be the same clip?

"David, what is it? Did you forget something?"

The girl grabbed her bag and continued outside and away from them.

"Hm? No." He resumed walking. "I was just deciding if I wanted burgers and fries."

"Well, decide quick. I don't have much time." Shelby was practically sprinting as they walked outside.

If he kept to her pace, they would pass the girl in shapely blue jeans and a snug knit top. He panicked. "Let's go to North Star instead," he suggested, knowing it would require them to head in a different direction.

"David," Shelby's voice boomed, "Come on. I'm hungry."

The girl suddenly halted and whirled around. David stopped, too, watching her every move. In that long-awaited moment, the mystery was solved. He'd know that face anywhere. She was even prettier than he remembered. Aliyah stood in front of him and Shelby flanked his side.

"Aliyah?" He still didn't trust himself.

Her eyes widened. "David?" she gasped.

"What are you doing here?"

Aliyah briefly glanced at Shelby. "I think it would be obvious," she answered with the same sarcasm so familiar to him.

This encounter had stirred Shelby's curiosity, and he anticipated her explosion. "Aliyah, this is Shelby." He turned to Shelby. "Aliyah is…an old friend."

Then, he asked Aliyah, "You were just in Professor Hartman's class, weren't you?"

"Yes." She cocked her head to the side, "I know, why does a girl with Israeli citizenship need to take a government class?" She shook her head. "It's a long story."

"I thought that was you."

~

David's more-than-likely girlfriend eyed Aliyah from head to toe with a smirk. "It's nice to meet you, Shelby," Aliyah offered, but all of her focus was on David, her old—*friend.*

"Yeah, you too," Shelby said, but Aliyah suspected she didn't mean it. Nothing mattered except the one whom Aliyah had pined for was within hugging distance, but there would be no hugging. He had gone on with his life, and this beauty was his girlfriend. A pain burned right beneath her heart.

"We're going to grab some burgers. Want to join us?" David asked.

Aliyah almost found herself mesmerized by his eyes—just as blue as she remembered. He was taller than she expected, lean but muscular, and she found herself struggling for air.

"No, thank you. I have a class," she lied. "We'll have to catch up some other time," she offered.

"Yeah, definitely."

As Aliyah left them, she couldn't have felt more hopeless. A tear escaped and she brushed it away. For a second, she wished for Tel Aviv and even found consolation in the thought of marrying Jacob Steiner but quickly remembered the freedom of being here.

That night, Aliyah tossed and turned in her bed. Her roommate texted most of the night, but not Aliyah. She couldn't stop thinking about seeing David with Shelby. *Of course, he is happy with a girl like that. What is there not to like about her? Besides, there is no future for us anyway.* She took a deep breath, rolled over on her back, and stared at the ceiling. All this time she had effectively kept her heart from all others, especially Jacob. But while she nursed a broken heart in Tel Aviv, David was with that blonde!

Well, hadn't she come for an education and not to see David? Aliyah knew she could tell herself that, but it wasn't the truth. The phone call to his house as soon as she'd arrived betrayed her.

Chapter Ten

Aliyah dreaded going to her government class on Thursday and seeing David with Shelby. She couldn't drop it because she needed the credit to keep her scholarships.

Only a few students entered the building in front of her as the class didn't start for another twenty minutes. Aliyah sat down in the middle of the third row and opened her book, hoping to bury her face in it. Too late. David walked through the door. Alone. He searched the room and their eyes met.

Aliyah's heart raced.

With determined strides, he closed the distance and took the seat next to hers. "I was hoping you'd be here a little early" His face reddened slightly, but he was handsome with his summer tan, rich brown, almost black hair, and baby blue eyes. Still—

"Oh? Where's your girlfriend?" She leaned forward and peered around him, trying not to let on how much he affected her.

"Shelby? She's not my girlfriend."

"What is she then? A 'friend?'" She changed her tone on the last word, acknowledging his previous reference to her.

"Well, technically she is…my girlfriend…uh…" he shook his head. "Do you know how shocked I was to see you?"

"You? What about me?" They stared at each other for seconds. "So, where's Shelby?"

"She dropped the course."

Aliyah nodded. She thought about this one class, the class she wasn't supposed to have, and yet here she was with David. At least, she wouldn't have to see Shelby anymore.

"Have you lived here all this time?" David asked.

She whispered because, one by one, students had filled the seats around them within eavesdropping distance. "No. Tel Aviv. I just arrived last Saturday."

"Why didn't you call me?"

"I did."

"When?"

"On Saturday."

Professor Hartman walked in and silenced everyone, commencing the class.

David pulled a spiral notebook out of his bag, opened it, and wrote, *No, I mean, why didn't you call, write, or email six years ago?* He slipped it to her for a response.

Aliyah stared at the page for a moment. How weirdly wonderful to be sitting here writing notes with David. She recalled doing this very thing, just the two of them all those years ago. She smiled at him and then remembered Shelby. She took the pen. *It's a long story, too long for a note.*

David replied. *Then let's get together. What's your phone number? Where are you staying?*

Aliyah thought for a second, then wrote, *Shelby*

might not like it.

He stared at her, and she fought the urge to look away, holding his gaze for seconds before he broke it to resume writing.

She doesn't control me. I can get together with a friend. She'll be fine with it.

A friend, Aliyah thought, *So, does he only think of me as a friend?* He had told her he loved her, but they were only twelve. Perhaps their relationship meant more to her than him. She wrote, *okay,* followed by her phone number and dorm assignment.

At the end of class, David asked, "Do you want to grab some lunch?"

She looked into his persuasive eyes. She wanted to say yes, but the last thing she wanted was to eat with David and Shelby. "No, I have a class, remember?" She started walking away.

~

David couldn't believe he'd finally found her, and she was being aloof. He called after her, "Can I call you this evening?"

She yelled over her shoulder. "I gave you my number, didn't I?"

His phone vibrated with a message from Shelby. *Cheer practice 2night & out w girls. C U tomorrow?*

OK, he responded, thankful that she wouldn't be contacting him.

After lunch, David had economics and a good amount of studying. His mood perplexed him. He didn't remember when he'd been this stoked. He could hardly wait until he could call Aliyah. After seeing her on Tuesday, it had been difficult to wait until class today.

David's roommate, Gage, was at football practice.

Players and cheerleaders alike were getting ready for the big game this Saturday. The quiet room made for optimal studying. David closed his book and tossed it on the others. He propped up a couple of pillows on his bed, picked up his cell, and plopped down on his back. His hand quivered a bit as he started to call.

Why couldn't he and Aliyah pick up where they left off? He knew the answer. She was different. He was different. It had been almost six years since he'd seen or heard from her. He'd played football through high school, worked hard at his studies, and dated some, mostly Shelby since the beginning of his senior year. She was homecoming queen; they'd gone to prom together. Shelby was beautiful, popular, and…she had filled a void, made him feel somewhat normal. After Aliyah left, it took him months to get over her. To believe her forever gone. He'd become goal-oriented and focused on the future. David knew nothing about Aliyah's years, but she had changed. He touched the call circle and he heard it ringing.

"Hello." He closed his eyes and his head fell back on the pillows. Her voice sounded so familiar, taking him back.

"Hi. Are you free? Is this a good time?"

"No. I have hot wax all over my legs and there's a fire down the hall." She talked fast and gasped for air.

"What? A fire?? Did you call 9-1-1?"

She giggled. "Aw, same as always, gullible DAVE!"

He laughed. "There it is—you haven't lost it—that dry sense of humor. And it's DAVID."

"How have you been…David?"

He took a deep breath, trying to think of where to start. "How do you catch up on six years at a time?"

"I guess slowly. We lived it one day at a time."

"Yeah. I thought about you a lot."

"Really? Was that before or after you started dating Shelby?"

"No, no, no. First, you answer my question."

"I didn't hear a question."

He stood and with one hand brushed his hair back. "Why didn't you call or write or email or something? You know, 'the long story?'"

"Oh, that one. How much time do you have?"

He couldn't see her, but he knew she was smiling. "I've got all night." He cradled his head in his free hand. Aliyah didn't speak and he waited before asking, "How was Tel Aviv?"

"It's different. My parents sent me to a private school." Again, there was silence.

"What was that like?"

She drew a deep breath. "I never had access to the internet."

"What kind of school did you go to?"

"An all-girls school."

He could tell she struggled to talk about it. "You want to go to dinner? There's a pizza place not far," he suggested. Perhaps she'd be more relaxed if they talked face-to-face.

She didn't answer at first. Then, "Okay." She sounded unsure, but he didn't give her time to rethink it.

He sprang to his feet. "I'll pick you up in ten." He barely heard her second okay before he hung up.

~

Aliyah stared at her phone. This was a bad idea. She should have said no. Still, she searched through her clothes, tossing the rejects aside, cluttering the floor.

Finally, she chose black leggings and glanced at the magenta knit top hanging in the closet and smiled. It had a low neckline and a narrow waist. She stepped into her black flats and checked the window just as a truck parked outside. Grabbing her bag, she dashed out the door.

David was standing on the sidewalk in front of his truck when she ran outside. He took her breath away. His thick brown hair was swept back with a wave in it and framed his tan face. He needed to shave, which only made him more distinguishable. His straight jeans accentuated his height. All grown up.

His eyes surveyed her, and he laughed. She immediately joined him. He wore a button-up shirt open over a magenta t-shirt. "We match." His eyes danced.

"How awkward is that?" she asked, smiling as he opened the door for her.

As he climbed behind the wheel, she couldn't remember when she'd felt this good. Almost, she believed she could right her world but knew better.

They entered the shop, ordered pizza, and sat at a table.

"Smells good," she offered.

He nodded, staring at her. She could feel the heat in her face when his eyes drifted below her chin. Her shirt revealed a hint of cleavage. It was a new style for her.

"So, how was it, going to an all-girls school?"

"Awful. Not the school, but the reason I went."

"I don't understand." He shook his head.

"David, you have never understood my family."

"You mean your weird family, and you're right."

"We're not weird. We're Jewish."

"Not all Jews are as strange as your family."

"I agree, but not all are as observant, either."

"So, you still haven't told me why you never contacted me."

The waiter delivered their pizza—half pepperoni and half cheese, all piping hot. David reached for her hand. "Will you pray with me?" He had never done that before, and for a second, she felt uncomfortable, but when she gave him her hand, a current flowed between them and her heart raced.

David bowed his head. "Dear Lord, thank you for this food and thank you for bringing my friend to Cornell. I don't always know why things happen, but you know the plans you have for me—for both of us. Bless this food and bless Aliyah. In Jesus' name, Amen."

When David released her hand, she couldn't comprehend her feelings. Again, he had referred to her as a 'friend.' For several seconds, she immersed herself with pizza.

David broke the silence. "After you left, every time the phone rang, I thought it might be you."

She stopped chewing and looked into his eyes. The honesty and hurt in them touched her.

"I constantly checked my email. Every day after school, I searched the mail. Surely, Aliyah will find some way to contact me, I thought, but you didn't."

"David, I tried. I wrote you a letter once. Before I could mail it, my parents found it. I got into big trouble." David shook his head, but she continued. "Do you remember that last day of school before I left? You kissed me."

David flushed. "How could I forget?"

"My mother…was in the car behind the bus."

"Oh, Aliyah. I'm sorry."

"They kept me pretty much in isolation after that. My

little sister and I became good friends. I actually welcomed going to school."

David placed his hand over hers, and Aliyah lost herself in the depth of his eyes. Neither of them noticed when a boisterous crowd of students entered through the door, until—

"David? What's this?"

Shelby stood beside their table. The other cheerleaders were ordering their pizza at the counter.

"Shelby, you remember Aliyah?"

Shelby cleared her throat and stared at his hand resting on Aliyah's. David jerked it away. Then, she scooted into the booth beside him and faced her.

"Yes, have you guys been catching up?" She helped herself to a slice of pizza.

David nodded. "That's right. We've been catching up." He glanced briefly at Aliyah, and she cocked her head to the other side.

Who is he trying to protect? Shelby or me? Aliyah couldn't compete with Shelby, especially in her cheerleader uniform, which accentuated her shapely figure. Makeup adorned her exquisite face and charming smile. Her long blond hair was pulled back in a bouncy ponytail.

Shelby grasped David's attention and she kissed his cheek lightly. "I'm sorry I had practice, Babe, but at least you had company."

Aliyah's stomach soured and she thought she might gag. She regretted her decision to come eat pizza. Going to college in the states might just be one of her biggest mistakes. "Well, I'd better leave you two alone and get back. It's getting late."

David objected, "No. I brought you here, Aliyah. I'll

take you home. Besides, you shouldn't be out by yourself after dark."

"David? You're not going to leave me, are you?" Shelby pouted as some of her friends sat at the table beside them. "I just ordered my pizza."

"Shel, you said you were going out with the girls." He placed a few bills on the table for a tip. "Have a good time." He motioned for her to let him out.

Aliyah was already on her feet. "Nice to see you again, Shelby."

"Yeah, you, too."

Aliyah witnessed Shelby kiss him again before she could turn and head for the door.

Once in the truck, David stared at the steering wheel. "I'm sorry about that."

"It's okay. Your life is different now. I understand."

"No." He started the engine. "You don't understand." He seemed to be searching for words and started to speak several times, but for the most part, they rode in silence. When the truck came to a stop outside her dorm, he asked, "What are you doing tomorrow night?"

"It's Shabbat. I'll be going to Shabbat dinner at the Center."

David nodded. "Well, what about the game on Saturday? Are you going?"

"I doubt it. It's Shabbat."

"When can we get together again?"

"I don't think it's a good idea." In fact, she knew it wasn't. "Good night, David." She slipped out of the truck and heard his door open. She ran down the sidewalk, up the steps, and through the door. He called after her, but she didn't stop. Once inside the sanctity of her room, she fell on the bed. *I must be insane.* Her phone chimed.

Why is it not a good idea? I want to see you. You owe me that for not contacting me. I missed you.

She pondered how she should answer. *David, if we continue to disobey my parents, we'll only get hurt. I don't want to hurt you.*

I'm willing to take that chance. I care that much. Do you? Do you care about me at all?

What, as a FRIEND?

Yes...and much more.

She closed her eyes and smiled. He cared about her as much more than a friend. *What am I doing? I must stop this now for both of our sakes.* She sighed, picked up her phone, and texted. *David, I'm just here for school. When I graduate, I'll return home and marry Jacob Steiner.*

What?

When she didn't answer, her phone chimed again. *I suppose I should have asked you if there was someone else. Do you love him?*

He's a nice Jewish boy. I think we can make a life together.

Is that what you want? Is he who you want?

Good night, David. I'll see you on Tuesday.

Aliyah remained in her clothes and pulled the sheet up over her. She touched her phone and "Chasing Cars" played.

She stared at nothing and let tears roll unbidden to her pillow. That's what she wanted—just to spend time, anytime, with David. Did she dare?

Chapter Eleven

Saturday morning, David awoke after a night of restlessness. He supposed it was possible that Aliyah didn't love him as he loved her, but he refused to accept it. He felt something when they were together and he believed she did, too. He intended to fight, but he needed help. He picked up his phone.

~

Birds sang in the sun as a soft breeze caressed Beth's skin. She sat in her patio chair, sipping coffee and reading her Bible. Phil read the Saturday morning paper across the table from her. Beth finished her devotion and eyed him as he was engrossed in his reading. "You know, I've been thinking about your suggestion."

Phil peered above his paper, and having secured his attention, she continued. "Celebrating our twentieth wedding anniversary in Milan sounds wonderful."

He abandoned the paper altogether. "Oh, honey, we'll have a great time. We've never really had any alone time of our own. This is our chance."

She smiled at him. His exuberance was contagious and exciting.

"Did Melissa say something when she called this

morning that helped you change your mind?"

"Not really. She talked about this young man on campus. Apparently, he texted her and asked her to pray about being his girlfriend." She shook her head. "I just think that's the sweetest story…the wisest suggestion…he sounds positively perfect."

Phil placed his hand over hers. "We prayed for God to prepare and send the perfect mate for our children and He will."

"I know, and with Melissa doing well at Harvard and David off to Cornell." She smiled coyly and approached his chair. "They have their lives. We'll be there for them—" she pulled him to his feet and stepped into his embrace. "—but it's okay for us to go live ours."

He kissed her, stirring her desire. She whispered against his lips, "We could go inside and be more intimate."

He smiled. "I knew there'd be perks to the kids leaving the nest."

She turned to run inside and squealed when he chased after her. The phone rang, of course, at that inopportune time. She yelled, "don't answer it."

Phil had already glanced at caller ID. "It's David. I'd better take it."

Beth raced back to his side. "Yes., yes. Answer it."

"Hello."

Beth's adrenaline rushed. Her independent little boy was calling home. She tried to hear and ended up hanging on Phil's arm, anxious to learn the reason for his call.

"Hi, son. How's it going up there?"

Beth thought about rushing for the extension, but then she might miss something.

"No, we're not busy." Phil looked at Beth as he answered. "Today?" He paused. "Sure, we can spend the night and go with you to church tomorrow."

"What?" Beth whispered, but Phil raised his pointer finger.

"Okay. We'll see you in four to five hours."

When Phil hung up, Beth couldn't stand the suspense. "What? What's happened?"

"Nothing." He took her face in his hands. "He says everything is fine, but he needs advice," his voice elevated some, "from us! Our son is asking for advice from his parents, believe it or not. He doesn't want to talk about it over the phone."

"I can't believe it. He went from not wanting us to take him to college to please come and give me advice." Beth's shock didn't remove her curiosity. "I wonder what in the world is wrong."

"He mentioned he wants us to go to church with him." Phil was deep in thought. "You know, I don't think we should drive. Let me see if I can get a helicopter."

Beth agreed before rushing inside to pack a small bag. What had prompted David to call for help? This was not like him at all.

~

The helicopter landed on their property thirty minutes later, and they were ready. The ride shook Beth's stomach to the point of nausea, but the New England countryside with rich green fields and full trees that stretched to the sky took her breath away. Only a few of the leaves had started changing.

David met them at the helipad in Ithaca. "Mom, you look a little green."

Beth reached out her hand and leaned on his

shoulder. "I'll be alright in a minute."

The three of them climbed in David's pickup and headed back to town. Her son turned and smiled briefly at them.

"Thanks for coming," he said.

Despite the smile, frown lines framed his eyes and cheeks, which signaled desperation, a look perhaps only recognizable by a mother.

Phil responded, "You knew we'd be here."

"I know. You guys have always been there, dad."

"What's all this about?" Beth couldn't relax until she knew what was going on with her son.

David took a deep breath. "There's a football game today. Big Red is playing at home. Shelby's on the field…and I'm not there."

"Why not?" Phil asked. Beth remained quiet and let Phil take the lead.

"You see, that's just it. There's something more important…well…someone."

Beth knew Shelby wasn't the right girl for David, but had he found someone else within the first week of school?

"Do you remember Aliyah from middle school?"

Did she remember? How could she forget? "Yes…the little girl who moved to Tel Aviv?"

David took his eyes off the road and glanced at her and Phil. "She's here."

Phil jumped to conclusions. "Is that the reason you wanted to come to Cornell?"

David's eyes widened. "What? No. I hadn't heard from her." With a calmer voice, added, "but I never stopped loving her."

"Oh, my goodness," Beth exclaimed. "It must have

been her. The girl who called on the Saturday you left. She hung up without telling me her name."

"Yes, that was her. I know you guys didn't think I was old enough to be in love, but—"

"Well, David," Phil started in a 'let's be logical' tone, "how old were you when she left, twelve or thirteen?"

"I knew, son," Beth admitted. "You pined for years after she left. You searched the mail every day."

"So, why are *we* here?" Phil asked.

"Aliyah and I have one class together. You want to hear something crazy? She didn't even sign up for it. Aliyah tried to drop it and couldn't. We went out the other night. I still feel the same about her, and I believe she does, too."

"That's great," Phil and Beth both chimed in at the same time.

"No, it's not."

When David stopped talking, Phil prompted, "What's the problem?"

"She's Jewish, and her parents have some kind of hold on her."

Beth felt her son's pain and knew his dilemma. "David, both Jews and Christians believe you're to honor your father and mother."

"I know, but her parents are unreasonable."

David parked in the lot for Rudy's Fine Dining in Ithaca.

"I take it we're going to eat here?" Phil asked.

"My dorm isn't the right place to have this conversation. Maybe we can talk in privacy here. I looked it up on the internet."

After the waiter took their order, Beth asked, "David, have you prayed about this?"

"I have Mom…for many years. I'm not sure if Aliyah has always known, but I have always known that I love her."

"Well, David, if you're talking about a soulmate," Phil said, "you'll find that God wants you to choose someone of your own faith."

"I'm a Christian and he doesn't want me to choose a non-Christian—is what you're saying."

"Exactly."

"But, Dad, you weren't a Christian when Mom married you."

Phil glanced at Beth for reassurance. "We weren't exactly in God's will, either. Are you?"

"I'm trying to be."

Phil asked. "Is Aliyah a Christian?"

David's head leaned to the side and his lips formed a straight line. His eyes glazed with sorrow.

"Have you tried talking with her about her faith?" Beth asked.

"Not really, but some. Aliyah has connected with the Jewish Center here on campus. Her religion is important to her. I spent last night learning everything I could about Judaism, and honestly, it's really confusing."

"It is," Phil agreed. "I've studied the difference between Judaism and Christianity some, and Judaism is quite complex."

The waiter served their food, and Phil reached for David's and Beth's hands. "Dear Lord, thank you for your abundance to us. Bless this food we are about to eat. Lord, may we ever be mindful to seek your will first and allow you to guide us. We ask this in the blessed name of Jesus, Amen."

David's fork remained on the table. "You see, I think

it is God's will for me to share my faith with Aliyah; it might free her. You know, Mom, like you're always saying, 'the truth will set you free.'"

Beth thought hard and she knew Phil was, too. "Yes, but you're walking on thin ice," she began. "Aliyah does need to know the Truth." She took a deep breath and let it out slowly. For the first time, Beth realized the trap that held her son. An impossible love. *Oh God, don't let him get hurt again. If Aliyah is the one, then prepare a pathway for them and show her the truth.*

Phil took over. "You realize—you could be asking her to choose between you and her parents?"

"No. I don't want to come between her and her parents. That's her family."

"I hope you do introduce Aliyah to Jesus but know her parents are not going to like it, and they may never accept you."

"But aren't we supposed to leave our mother and father? How's it written…'cleave unto each other and become one flesh?'" he pleaded.

Phil looked at Beth, his eyebrows furrowed. He placed his hand on David's shoulder. "Let's talk to the pastor at your church here and see if he can counsel you on a plan of action. Trust God, son. It'll work out."

"It has to, Dad."

They ate in silence for a while. Beth knew David was frustrated and desperate. She and Phil had gone to religion classes back when David was younger, and Aliyah still lived here. When their second grader told them he was in love, and they learned her parents wouldn't let her play with him, they decided they needed to understand more about the Jewish faith. When Aliyah left the country, David was heartbroken, but maybe God was separating them for a reason. Now, what a twist of fate. Not only was Aliyah back in the states, but in the very same school as David, and they had been placed in the same class together, one Aliyah wasn't even supposed to have.

"There's more." David didn't look at either of them. "She's supposed to marry this guy back in Israel."

Beth practically choked on her bite. She took a drink of her iced tea.

"She is? Aw, David." Phil sounded as if he understood the futility of the situation. "A nice, upstanding, promising Jewish young man?"

"I assume." David hung his head.

Beth squeezed his arm. "We'll pray and let God work."

~

David drove his parents around town past the church he attended, and Phil wrote down the name of the pastor. They went by the Jewish Center and David searched the people he saw, hoping one of them would be Aliyah.

Shelby called late that afternoon as his parents were checking into a hotel. "David. Where were you?"

"My parents flew into town and I had to pick them up. We've been seeing the sights." His mom gave him a look of understanding.

"You missed my stunt," Shelby pouted. "Are you going to invite me over or what?"

"Not today, Shel. They're checking into a hotel right now. We've some family things to discuss."

"Well, okay, but—"

"Let's get together tomorrow afternoon," he suggested, knowing that he needed to talk to her about their relationship. She wouldn't be going to church tomorrow. That was one of the things she liked about college—no parents to make her go.

"Okay."

When he hung up, he felt relieved to have a course of action planned. He needed to end things with Shelby if he was going to convince Aliyah to open her mind about her religion and him. Talking with his mom and dad gave him confidence, but it was also sobering.

The next morning, he picked up his parents and they went to worship at Faith Family Church. When they walked in, David noticed several college-age students in attendance. He and his mom and dad found a seat in a pew not far from the front. The worship team consisted of a live band and a mixture of old and young people singing. The pastor, Reverend Tom Page, started his sermon.

"What does it mean to be in the world and not of the world?" the preacher began.

David usually took notes during the sermon, and today was no different. The sermon contained material he'd heard before as Pastor Page continued. With charisma, the preacher spoke eloquently and taught more than preached. David liked that. He listened for any word that God might have for him, a sign that would point him on the right path.

"Right here in Ithaca, New York, with Cornell University, young people are making decisions that affect their entire lives. It's important to consult the Word of God when you're talking about your whole life, amen?"

Several in the sanctuary uttered an amen, causing David to glance around.

"For example, many students will embark on lifelong

journeys and develop relationships. Some may be good; others may be harmful. They could be business-related, or they could be matters of the heart. Whatever they are, we know that God's Word gives direction in Second Corinthians 6:14. Let's turn there together."

David followed along as Pastor Page read, "Do not be unequally yoked together with unbelievers—" He didn't hear the rest because his eyes were glued to these words. David's heart pounded. As the pastor closed his sermon, a young woman came forward and sang God Will Make a Way. ♫♫♫ David fought tears as he listened to the words. Every single word was meant specifically for him.

After the service, the three of them went forward and David's dad introduced himself, Beth, and David to Pastor Page. He was attentive and agreed to meet with David twice a week to pray and discuss the right actions for him to take.

After David dropped his parents back at the airport, Shelby called him. "Yep. I'm on my way to pick you up," he said. "I thought we'd go to the park."

"The park?" Shelby grunted. "I haven't seen you all weekend."

"I know, but there's something I want to talk to you about. I thought we'd go check out Ithaca Falls."

"Okay. It might be fun."

Shelby's idea of fun and David's idea were two different things. Breaking up with Shelby wouldn't be easy, but he had to take care of this now.

When he picked her up, she was out on the lawn in shorts talking and, from what he could tell, flirting with the boys throwing a football. She ran to the truck and hopped in. Shelby scooted close and kissed him without seeming to notice he wasn't kissing her back. She waved out the window as they drove away.

"What did you and your parents talk about?"

"It's kind of personal." It was a small deception, but he needed more time to prep for his announcement.

"I'm glad you're here now. I haven't been to the falls, have you?" She placed her hand on his thigh.

"Nope. You can take some pictures." He smiled at her, then turned his eyes on the road ahead. When they parked and climbed out, he joined her and took her hand in his. They walked in green grass, the sound of the falls nearby. Birds darted from tree to tree. As they strolled along the water, David began, "Shelby, how long have we dated?"

"About a year now. Remember? You asked me out just before homecoming."

David stared at the ground and grimaced. This really wasn't going to be easy. He stopped and put his hand in his pocket because he needed to steady his nerves.

Shelby misread that action. She shrieked and jumped up and down. "Oh, David. You're going to pop the question!"

His mouth dropped. He shook his head. "No! I'm not."

Shelby frowned. "Oh. You said you wanted to talk about something."

"I do, Shel. I—" he took a deep breath. "I think we should take a break. We're both changing and deciding what we want. Our future is still being shaped. We should see other people." He watched Shelby deflate before him, her eyes brimming with tears.

"This has to do with that girl from Israel, doesn't it?"

He fought the urge to lie and wrap his arms around

her in comfort. "I could say no, but I'd be lying."

She hit his chest with her fists and broke into sobs.

He clasped her in his strong arms. "I'm sorry, Shelby. I really am."

Shelby pulled away, sniffing. Then, she composed herself but refused to look at him. "You can take me back now."

Those were the last words she said to him before he dropped her back at her dorm. "Shelby," he called out to her as she closed the door, but she didn't look back.

When he returned to his room, he decided to call his sister in Boston.

"Well, hi there, little brother," she answered.

"Hi, Mel."

"So, how do you like it at Cornell?"

"It's fine. I broke up with Shelby today," he told her.

"You did what?"

"Yeah." he raked his fingers through his hair and sat on the bed.

"It was only a matter of time."

"Oh yeah? I'm glad somebody knew."

"She's too immature for you. I mean, she's pretty and all, but is that—"

David interrupted her. "Mel, Aliyah is here."

"Whoa! At Cornell?"

"Yes. We have a class together. Her parents let her leave Israel and come to school here."

"Did you know she was coming?"

"What's with everybody? No. We ran into each other in a class that—get this—a class she's not even supposed to have."

"David, that sounds like a God thing."

That brought a smile to his face.

"I hope it works out," she added.

He sighed. "We'll see."

David told her about his time with Aliyah and asked her to pray that God would reveal the truth to her. He explained how Aliyah's Jewish faith might separate them forever.

"I think you're meant to be together, or God wouldn't have brought the two of you to the same campus."

"Thanks. I hope you're right." He closed his eyes and stretched out on his bed. "So, what about you? How are things at Harvard?"

He listened to Melissa tell him about a boy named Scott whom she met at a Christian thing on campus, how before he even asked her out, he texted her and asked her to pray about being his girlfriend. When David hung up, he felt challenged but at peace. He had much to think about before falling asleep tonight.

Chapter Twelve

Aliyah hadn't slept well since going out with David. She had gone to Shabbat services, but she fretted all weekend long. Papers were due on Monday, and she couldn't focus on her assignments. Thoughts of David occupied her mind. She should never have come back to the states. Why didn't she stay in Israel and prepare to be the wife of Jacob Steiner? So, what if she didn't love him. What did love have to do with anything? She'd always been taught that everything was about obligation.

It didn't matter how much she reasoned—Aliyah Zimmerman loved David Drake. That was a fact she couldn't erase or deny. How could she live her life without him, especially after seeing him again?

Tuesday morning arrived just as sure as time marched on. Aliyah's alarm sounded and she turned it off. She rolled over and stared at the ceiling, inhaled and exhaled, then tossed her comforter aside. Walking to the bathroom, she stepped over her roommate's nightclothes. An empty cereal box teetered on the side of the sink and fell to the floor. She looked at herself in the mirror as she reached for her toothbrush. Her hair was a mess. With toothbrush in hand, she backed up and took a second look at her face. Her fingers outlined the dark circles around her eyes, the result of sleepless nights.

With backpack in hand, Aliyah headed for McGraw Hall and government class. Somehow, she'd have to avoid David. Without realizing it, Aliyah increased her pace, and her heart betrayed her. She scaled the steps, eager to see the one she loved.

When Aliyah entered the room, she saw him halfway up and in the middle. She thrilled at the sight of him. *What am I doing? Am I that weak that I'd eagerly break both of our hearts all over again?* Hers would always be broken, but his didn't have to be. She stopped two rows in front of him and took a seat in the middle. How awful it was being this close and having to keep distant.

Moments later, he joined her. Her pulse raced and she couldn't help being overjoyed, yet she stared ahead. "What are you doing, David? I told you I'm supposed to get married."

"I'm sitting by a—" he gestured with air quotes, "'— friend.'"

She stared at him, trying to think of something rude to say, but all she could do was delight in the sight of him. His smile, the single wave in his hair, the broad shoulders that filled out his navy-blue Under Armour sport shirt, his jean-clad, long legs and trim waist.

He sat down beside her. "So, how was Shabbat?"

She smiled. "How was the game?"

"I think we lost."

She nodded and imagined him in the stands, watching Shelby cheer and do whatever she did while the football players were getting their butts kicked, for she'd already heard the runaway score of their opponents.

"I broke up with Shelby yesterday," he whispered in her ear.

She jerked her head around. He was so close. Their eyes met; their mouths only five inches apart. "You did?" She broke the trance. "Oh, David, no."

He leaned back and shrugged. "It was going to happen anyway. I was never going to marry her, not like you and…what's his name?"

"Jacob?"

"What's up with that anyway? Do you love him?"

Professor Hartman walked in and all chatter stopped. David reached into his bag and pulled out the notebook. He raised his eyebrows. She whispered a giggle.

So, do you love him? He slipped her the notebook.

What's love got to do with it?

Everything! If you don't love him, I doubt you can build a life together. But if you do, then that's a different story.

She decided to change the subject. *Shabbat was good. I like the Jewish Center. Everyone is friendly there.*

You're avoiding the question.

You wouldn't understand. It's a Jewish thing.

David's jaw clenched and his face sobered. He appeared to be earnestly listening to Professor Hartman. She turned her attention to class, suspecting she may have offended him. In a moment, David's notebook nudged her arm. She looked down and took it.

You're right. I've been trying to understand the Jewish thing. Maybe I could go with you sometime?

The suggestion surprised her. *Okay, how about this Shabbat?*

Sure, but I'll want to know what we're doing and why. Fair?

Agreed. She hadn't considered that David might convert to Judaism. If David would convert to Judaism, her parents might accept him. Still, they wouldn't be happy about her breaking her promise to marry Jacob.

~

After class, they walked out together. "Want to grab a bite to eat?" David asked.

"Sure," she answered without hesitation.

David stopped. "Wait. Don't you have a class?"

"I just told you that, Dave." She kept walking.

He jogged a couple of steps to catch up and tickled her on each side, feeling the tiny spans of her waist beneath her loose-fitting t-shirt. Shaking his head, "It's DAVID, and that's something else you have to add to your list of wrongdoings."

"What?"

"Lying."

She stopped and turned on him, her ponytail flying around to the front. "I didn't lie. I just…" she hesitated. "Besides, there was no harm done."

David laughed. "Right. Tell that to God. You do believe in the Ten Commandments, right?"

"Of course, I do. They were written for *my* people."

David decided to let that one go. He would relish his accomplishment of being invited to Shabbat services and sharing lunch with Aliyah.

They ambled together side by side under the warm sun to the Cornell dining hall. With tray in hand, they found a table away from others. "So, after Shabbat, do you have any plans this holiday weekend?" he ventured.

Her eyes widened and she gasped. "Oh, David, I'm sorry. We can't go to Shabbat together. I have to go to the city. I'm supposed to spend the weekend with relatives there."

Disappointment replaced optimism within David until he thought again. "Maybe I can go with you. I know people there, so it's not like I wouldn't have a place to stay." David took a bite of his hamburger.

"Oh, that's right your grandparents live there, don't they? How is your grandfather? Is he…" her voice trailed off.

David nodded. "Yes, he's doing okay, now. His cancer came back, and he had to go through more radiation, but they did surgery and then chemo. He's as ornery as ever, but Mom says he's different."

"Do you think you could stay with him?"

"I'm sure. He's still trying to talk me into aeronautical design."

"Really?"

"I don't think he understands that it just might not be my thing. So, when do you want to meet and where?"

She paused and stared at the table before answering. "Well, I can tell my aunt and uncle I want to go shopping or something. We'll just have to be super careful. If my parents found out, it could be really bad."

David understood only too well. Would the two of them always have this shadow hanging over them, forever separated by a canyon of religion and ethnicity? Could he ever destroy that barrier?

She smiled and her eyes gleamed. "But I could call you on Sunday and we can decide then where to meet."

"Yeah, but you'd have to lie to your aunt and uncle." David remembered his father asking him if he was living in God's will.

The smile left her face at his five-word statement. "Telling them the truth isn't an option."

"You go. I'll see you when you return."

She was quiet the rest of lunch. David dreaded asking anything for fear she'd reject him, but he took a deep breath. "So, want to see the botanical gardens tonight?"

Her face lit up. "I have class until five. I can after that."

"Okay, I'll pick you up at six."

"Wait. Get out your green notebook."

He searched his backpack. "Why?"

Her brown eyes sparkled. "You'll see."

He handed it to her, and she opened it to the current page and began writing. When she returned it, he read, *What color shirt are you going to wear tonight*?

David chuckled as he fondly remembered their dress collaboration at the school dance. *Why*? *Do you plan on wearing a matching one*?

No. I want to make sure we don't match.

"Yeah, it might be weird if we showed up wearing the same thing," he told her. "It was great in middle school, but…you know."

She nodded, and they gathered their things ready to go their separate ways.

~

It was still daylight savings time, so the sun hung in the sky a little longer. At dusk, the gardens closed, so Aliyah rushed back to her dorm after her class. She changed clothes, brushed her teeth and hair, and applied some lip gloss.

At quarter to six, she sat on the steps, waiting and thinking. Did she dare raise her hopes, or would hers be another story like Cinderella with the clock ticking, knowing that the carriage would eventually turn back into a pumpkin? She knew what she should do—knew she should obey her parents, knew she should marry Jacob, and yet, she couldn't prevent the way she felt.

David pulled over and parked at the curb. Aliyah's heart leapt, and she rushed to the pickup. She climbed in, closed the door, and burst out laughing. He was wearing a Big Red Cornell t-shirt and so was she.

"I guess I should have told you what I was going to wear." He chuckled.

She shook her head. "Nope. It's perfect." She slipped her hand into his and felt like she was floating in the clouds. He gently squeezed it, and she couldn't stop smiling, nor did she want to. The CD in his truck played a familiar song. She took a deep breath and rested her head on his shoulder. As she lost herself in the lyrics, she wanted to forget her world at home and spend time with David…forever.

"Did you know," David asked, "I live near a place called Falls Village, but I hardly ever go there? This place is filled with all these beautiful falls everywhere. Ironic, isn't it?" He pushed down on the accelerator. "Hopefully, we'll get there in time to make it to the falls."

David parked and they walked hand in hand along the walkways, passed by fragrant blooms, and strolled beneath wistful trellises with flowering vines. They didn't talk much. For Aliyah, it was enough just being together.

Drawing closer to the falls, David broke into a run across the green field, pulling her behind him. Finding the perfect spot, he lay down in the grass and she joined him. With hands clasped, they stared at the bluish-purple sky. The sun cast colors on the clouds and outlined them in shimmering gold highlights.

"It's beautiful," Aliyah said.

David was quiet and then, "That sky up there—it's our sky. Made just for us, just for this moment." They lay there for minutes before he rolled over on his side and leaned up on his elbow, staring at her.

Her face flushed from his scrutiny.

"I will never forget this time," he told her. "No matter what, I'll remember it always. And how beautiful you look lying here with your hair cascading around your head."

Aliyah lost herself in his gaze, enveloped in the love in his eyes. It felt right to caress his cheek with her fingers. When he drew closer, her heart raced, but it was the most natural thing when his lips joined hers. His were soft and lingered with tenderness, a fit so perfect they had to have been created for each other. As his arms pulled her closer, heaven encircled her. She never wanted him to let go.

As David pulled away, she read the pain in his eyes.

He shook his head. "I've longed for this. These past six years have been an eternity. I missed you so much."

A tear slipped down her cheek. In that instant, she knew. All the years of yearning for her so-much-more-than-a-best friend had been matched by his own. She wrapped her arms around him, "Oh, David." She kissed him again. "I thought it was probably puppy love. We were so young, and I knew we could never be, but I couldn't stop thinking about you, longing for you. Then when I saw you with Shelby—"

He placed his finger over her mouth. "There is no Shelby. There never really was." Aliyah could see the sincerity in his blue eyes. "She could never replace you. Just like the song says, you are all I have."

Aliyah heard the music with his words. He pulled her to her feet and into his strong embrace. He kissed her forehead and placed soft kisses in her hair. She clung to him, feeling refuge in the firmness and warmth of his chest. In that place and moment, she almost believed they could forget the world and stay here forever.

After leaving the gardens, David took her to dinner at Abraham's, a Kosher restaurant in town. She enjoyed their food, talked about old times, laughed, and too soon the night ended, leaving only the sobering reality of tomorrow.

Chapter Thirteen

After Aliyah's morning class, she caught a regional jet for the city, on her way to Uncle Levi and Aunt Sarah's place.

They greeted her with open arms. Aliyah's cousins, Jonathan, Eli, and Rebekah, ranged in ages from five to nine. They hugged her and tugged on her dress.

"That's enough," Aunt Sarah told them. "Let Aliyah come inside, and take her suitcase, Jonathan."

The family gathered to celebrate and observe Shabbat, and Aliyah found it sobering because it reminded her of who she was. At the start of Shabbat dinner, Sarah lit two candles and sang the blessing. Would there ever be a world where she, a religious Jewish girl, could coexist with David, a Christian? She knew the answer to that. Hopelessness weighed heavily.

Aliyah and Aunt Sarah were washing dishes on Sunday afternoon when Aliyah decided to ask, "Has anyone in our family ever married someone that wasn't Jewish?"

The question took Aunt Sarah by surprise for she swung around and stared at her.

~

Beth found herself singing while she made lasagna for her family, their favorite. Phil had gone to pick Melissa up at the airport, and soon David would drive his truck into the driveway, the home she and Phil had bought almost two decades ago when they had married to fight for custody of Melissa. Soon, her home would be filled with the voices of her family, and it would feel like old times when both of her children were younger. She would enjoy it for the better part of three days until Melissa and David returned to their schools late Monday afternoon.

The back door chimed as David entered. "Smells good in here, Mom."

As he passed by the markings on the door, she noticed he was the same height as he'd been at the beginning of summer. His growth had stopped, a bittersweet reminder that her baby was an adult. Beth dried her hands on her apron and rushed to wrap her arms around him. "You look so handsome, just like your dad. Oh, I missed you so much."

"Wow, Mom. It's only been two weeks."

"I know, but it seems like forever. Sit down and tell me all about school…and Aliyah." Pointing toward the den, she took her apron off and hung it on the hook. They sat, she on one end of the sofa, he on the other. "So, how are you doing in all your classes?"

"Good." He nodded.

When he didn't elaborate, she touched his hand. "I'm so glad you're here."

He smiled. "Me, too, Mom. So, where's Dad?"

"He and Melissa are on their way home from the airport. They'll be here soon, but how's everything going with Aliyah?"

David took a deep breath and blew it out. "I'm working on it." He abruptly rose. "Well, I'm going to go put my stuff in my room." He kissed her on the forehead and walked away despite her disappointment.

In a few minutes, Phil and Melissa entered through the front door. Melissa's smile accentuated her dimples and her face glowed. She rushed across the floor, her smooth, long, black hair bouncing with each step. Beth had a flashback of the first time they brought Melissa home from court that fateful day. What joy her little girl expressed at the sight of her new home and toys, and what joy she had given them ever since that day.

Beth hugged her tight, then glanced at Phil. Except for a few extra lines in his face and an occasional strand of gray, he looked just the same, smiling the same as when they'd brought Melissa home twenty years ago.

"Oh, Mom, I have so much to tell you, but first, where's David?" With exuberant energy, Melissa sprang to the banister before Beth answered. "He's in his room."

Phil put his arm around Beth's shoulder, and they watched their daughter race upstairs.

~

When David entered his room, he immediately went for the box under his bed. He'd stashed it there to prevent his mom from seeing it. David rifled through the contents, picked up the gift box with the opal ring, but then dropped it back with the other contents. Deciding to take the notebook and cologne back to school with him, he removed them before replacing the box to its usual spot on his closet shelf. He pushed play on his stereo and Snow Patrol's CD filled the room with songs that stirred his soul with hope. He stared out his bedroom window at the ducks swimming in the pond below.

There was a loud knock and his door swung open as Melissa burst inside. "Give your sister a hug and tell me all about Aliyah." When he hugged her, she added, "Oh, I remember this music. You used to listen to it all the time. It was right after Aliyah left." She sat down Indian-style on his bed in her white shorts and blue top.

He nodded and sat down beside her. "'Chasing Cars'—that's our song," he admitted. "We've been spending some time together." He shook his head, feeling the intensity. Staring at his sister, he confessed, "I love her, Mel."

"I know. I knew when you gave her the ring."

"As hard as she was to reach then, I fear she may be even harder now."

Phil appeared at the door and smiled at them. "Ah, my children." He spread his arm in a wide-sweeping gesture, palm up with theatrical flair. "Dinner is served."

~

They sat in their usual chairs and Phil asked the blessing. Beth had set bowls of salad at each place and David reached for the main dish. "I've missed your lasagna, Mom."

"Yeah, this is great," Melissa chimed in while passing the bread.

Beth sat quietly, listening to the clinking of utensils and relished the sight of her family together around the table. Phil smiled at her and silently acknowledged her thoughts.

"Your mom and I are going to Milan for our anniversary," he announced. "We leave on Tuesday."

David and Melissa put their forks down. "That's great," Melissa said first.

"Yeah," David agreed. "I'm glad you two are doing

something special. After all, without you, we wouldn't be here." His response sounded forced.

"We may even spend some time in Paris," Phil added, to Beth's surprise. She would have said something but was more concerned about the reaction, or lack of, from their children.

"How long will you be gone?"

"Why do you ask, David?" Beth quietly responded.

"It's just that we usually spend 9/11 in New York with Uncle Jack, Aunt BJ, and Tyler. He's turning eleven this year. Aren't they having a birthday party for him?"

"I talked to Aunt BJ the other day and they're taking Ty to Universal Studios in Orlando this year." Beth stared at her son. Why was their leaving bothering him?

Phil speared bites of salad with his fork, "I know we're usually all together, but Mom and I haven't had any time away alone. Besides, we're all getting older and things are changing."

Melissa was staring at her brother as if she knew something the rest of them didn't.

"Why? Is this a bad time? Do you guys need us?" Beth asked.

"No." David shook his head. "Of course, not. You guys have a great time and take lots of pictures." He chowed down bites of lasagna, salad, and bread.

"You deserve it, Mom, Dad," Melissa agreed.

After a few moments, David divulged, "That's our anniversary—9/11—when I met Aliyah for the first time in the second grade."

"David, I never knew that," Phil said.

"We can put our trip off," Beth offered. "We could go next year."

Phil raised his eyebrows, sending her warning

signals. "How are things with you and Aliyah?" he asked.

"I broke up with Shelby, and Aliyah and I have gone out, but there's still this barrier."

"Have you met with Pastor Tom?"

"Yes, we've looked at scriptures and researched the Tanakh some, but Aliyah is pretty religious."

Beth marveled at how easily David opened up when questioned by his dad. She'd tried to get him to talk earlier, but he hadn't cooperated.

David continued. "She has agreed to take me to Shabbat services with her."

Beth choked on her wine and Phil dropped his bread in his lap. Beth hadn't anticipated her son subjecting his faith to trial.

"Don't worry. I'm not going to convert to Judaism." David rolled his eyes. "I figure if I go with her, then I can talk her into going with me."

Beth touched his sleeve. "I hope so, son." An awkward silence existed before Beth rose. "I made chocolate cake. Anyone want a piece?"

The three of them practically answered in unison.

~

Beth had slipped into her nightgown and finished brushing her teeth. Phil sat in bed reading. When she crawled between the sheets, she decided to talk to him about what had been bothering her since dinner. "What do you think about David going to Shabbat—that's the Sabbath, right? With Aliyah?"

Phil closed his book and placed it on the night table. "It shocked me." He put his arm around her, pulling her closer to him. "I guess he didn't hear what we said about being unequally yoked. He'll get emotionally attached before he knows it."

Beth couldn't believe Phil's naiveté. She sat up and looked at him. "Phil, our boy is already attached. He's been attached since the second grade when he sat on the barstool and asked me how old you had to be to fall in love."

Phil stared at her. "What can we do?"

"We need to wisen up. Our son is in over his head."

Phil looked pensive. "We'll have to keep praying."

~

Aliyah boarded the plane bound for Ithaca. She had three hours to contemplate her predicament. *Honor your father and mother*—she'd been taught that since she could talk. *Thou shalt not lie*—that one, too. Even David mentioned that. She hadn't seen the error in her ways before, like how wrong it was to lie to her parents about whom she was going to see, in order to steal moments with David. Or deceiving them, making them believe she was doing something else. When she continued to see David despite her parents' objection, she had disobeyed.

David had told her he wanted to go to Shabbat service. What if he converted to Judaism? Aunt Sarah's jaw dropped when Aliyah asked if anyone in the family had ever married outside their faith. She had studied the floor for seconds, then answered, "I don't think so."

If David converted, her parents would still believe she had deliberately come to America for one reason, and they'd feel she'd disobeyed them. They'd probably become more insistent she marry Jacob.

Aliyah sighed and dug her earplugs out of her bag. After selecting the music on her phone, the melody played. She closed her eyes and leaned her head back against the seat, refusing to think about her impossible love, losing herself in the music. She wished they didn't need her parents' or anyone's approval in order for them to be together, but she knew better.

~

David turned left on I-88, deep in thought, his Snow Patrol CD playing in the pickup. He couldn't wait to get back to Cornell and Aliyah. He felt thankful to have found her again and wasn't sure how, but he'd find a way for the two of them to be together always. He just had to.

Having never met her parents and knowing little about the Jewish religion, he felt ill-equipped, but he would learn, and by the grace of God, he would find a way.

His phone chimed and he glanced at it. The text was from Aliyah. He shouldn't drive and text, but it could be important.

Hope you had a great time with your family. I'm back on campus now. Am tired. I'll see you in Govt tomorrow.

He texted back sad faces. David wasn't sure what to make of her message. He only hoped that being with her family hadn't persuaded her to abandon her relationship with him. Either way, he'd have to wait until tomorrow to find out.

Chapter Fourteen

Shabbat, September 7th, 2012

David buttoned his shirt and tied his black tie in front of the mirror. Glancing at his phone, the time read six o'clock. Aliyah had talked with him at length about what would happen at dinner tonight. His palms sweat and his heart raced, but he bounced out of the house and down the steps. He didn't want them to be late. He and Aliyah were planning to walk to the Center because driving wasn't allowed during this time.

Aliyah was waiting on the sidewalk. Her long hair crowned her beauty, and her purple dress flowed loosely to just above her knees. She smiled and he took in the sight of her, her rosy cheeks and flawless olive complexion.

"Look at you," she crooned. "You dress up nice, tie and all."

"Like it?" He turned around three-sixty.

With a teasing grin, she tossed her head to the side. "You'll do."

He chuckled and took her hand. "And you look good in purple." He leaned close to her ear. "But then you always look good."

"Flattery will get you…well, it might get you

somewhere."

His phone dinged, and she turned to him alarmed. "You have to silence your phone. There's no technology on Shabbat."

"Where are you guys, still in the dark ages? It sounds cultic."

"David, I told you the Sabbath is a day of rest. It's a time to rejoice and enjoy each other and God's creation."

He silenced his phone and they continued walking. "So, when do I get one of those little beanie things for my head?"

She laughed. "It's called a *yarmulke*, and they'll give you one when we get there."

When Aliyah laughed, her eyes sparkled, and the world seemed right. He put his arm around her and enjoyed being close. If he had his way, he'd spend all of his time with her. David hoped his nerves didn't betray him. The closer the two of them got to their destination, the more nervous he became.

She squeezed his hand, and he searched her eyes. Their brown depths gleamed and held such warmth and understanding, giving him the courage he needed.

"Okay, so, can you go over everything one more time?" he asked.

"You're overthinking it. Relax. We begin with the lighting of the candles. Then we say the *Kiddush* prayer over the wine, then we wash our hands before breaking the *challah* bread."

"Oh, that's right. Tell me again how I wash them?"

"It's three times: once up, once down, and then up again. And get your whole hand wet. Then rub them together and dry but hold them chest high and don't speak until after the blessing has been recited."

David took a deep breath and blinked hard. "And you think my religion is tough."

"I don't think it's tough," Aliyah said nonchalantly. "I think it's wrong."

David abruptly stopped. "Wrong? How can you judge? Do you know anything about Christ?"

Her jaw dropped. They stood under an oak tree; its branches sprawled out over the walk. "I'm sorry. I didn't mean anything. It's just Jesus—"

"Jesus what?"

"Nothing. Please, forget I said anything." She tugged at his arm. "We're going to be late."

He fell into step. This was going to be much harder than he anticipated.

When they arrived, a large number of people milled around. Some of the men had long hair and beards but not all. Most dressed for every day, yet others wore nicer attire. They entered single file into the center, and one of the men gave David the customary head-covering. A young woman ceremoniously lit the candles, waving her hands in front of her face three times like she was inviting the light unto her eyes. On the third time, she covered her eyes with her hands and then removed them. Something graceful in this ritual captured David's attention.

He glanced at Aliyah who was on the other side of the room with the other women. Her face glowed with a beauty that came from within. It touched and moved him. She saw him and smiled. He couldn't look away. *God, you brought us together for a reason. I trust your purpose in it.*

When the rabbi started singing in Hebrew, it startled him. He watched with genuine curiosity as the evening unfolded. When the time came, he washed his hands, holding them chest level, and remained quiet until after the blessing. The two loaves of challah bread were broken, and he couldn't remember when he'd seen so much food.

Aliyah joined him as he was about to pass on the whole fish, which stared at him from a platter of sauce with sliced boiled eggs, adorned with some kind of greens and carrots.

"You'll want to try that," she whispered. "It's gefilte fish, a Jewish delicacy for Shabbat."

Against David's better judgment, he dipped a small portion of the fish onto his plate. Many had prepared dishes for this feast before this evening because no one was allowed to cook once the Sabbath began. He recognized most of the vegetables but hadn't seen them prepared in quite this way.

The food was delicious. Everyone welcomed him and made him feel comfortable. David constantly looked to Aliyah for reassurance but sometimes she would be missing. Then, he'd find her in the company of a young man named Michael, to whom he'd been introduced earlier. Michael often stared in Aliyah's direction.

When they walked home, she expressed her approval of the evening. "You were great, David. I think everyone forgot you weren't one of us." Her wide eyes and broad smile matched the laughter in her voice. She turned and walked backward, facing him. "But, oh, you should have seen your face when you saw the gefilte fish."

Her laugh was infectious, and he loved the way the moonlight shimmered on her hair. "So, how about that Michael guy?"

"Who?" She turned and slipped her hand inside his.

"You know, the guy with the glasses and sideburns who was always talking to you."

"Michael..." She wrinkled her nose. "I don't know his last name. We have a couple of classes together. He's new like me and doesn't have many friends."

"It's clear he wants to be your friend."

Aliyah punched David in the bicep before stopping and pulling away.

"What?" he protested.

"Are you jealous?"

He stared at her until he couldn't contain himself. Taking one step forward, he took her in his arms. "Yes," he admitted. "I'm jealous...jealous of Michael, jealous of your family, jealous of the Jewish religion. I'm jealous of anything that might take you from me."

She didn't speak, but their eyes locked. Finally, "Oh, David," she whispered. A tear rolled down her cheek.

David pulled her to his chest, his hand resting on her head. He never wanted to let her go for fear of tomorrow.

Shabbat, September 8th, 2012

Shabbat observance continued the next day with breakfast and a service in the morning. They met new people. How easy it would be for Aliyah to find all the support she needed right there. Toward the evening everyone gathered again for the Havdalah or evening service, which brought more wine and blessings in Hebrew and English. Verses recited throughout the day were the same as Old Testament scriptures he'd memorized, sometimes with a few variations, but he recognized them just the same.

The next morning, David didn't want to miss his

church service and afternoon appointment with Pastor Tom. During worship, he loved lifting his voice to praise the Savior. He sang, "Lord, you are the air that I breathe." David could not deny the beauty of observing Shabbat as he considered the contrasts between the two religious observances. Bridging the gap between himself and the girl he loved with all his heart seemed impossible.

~

Aliyah couldn't concentrate on her paper that was due the next day. She could only think about her desire to see David, but that would have to wait until tomorrow and government class with Professor Hartman. She and David would sit toward the back of the class and write in his notebook, just like they had as children. She didn't feel like that child anymore, but her parents still saw her that way. On that notebook, she could dream and plan and maybe even believe her dream would come true one day. She and David could hold hands and walk together and plan to meet at the park or attend a movie.

Then Aliyah made a decision. She would move boldly ahead and share the next four years with him, holding nothing back. She wanted him completely.

He had gone to Shabbat services with her, and for a while, she believed the two of them could be one someday. But in her Jewish world, David was forbidden fruit, and she was succumbing to temptation.

~

Tuesday, September 11, 2012

The next day, she raced to McGraw Hall and was disappointed to discover David wasn't there. She took her usual seat in the middle toward the back and anxiously stared at the door.

Professor Hartman walked in, set his briefcase down, and turned to the whiteboard. David slipped in and scaled the steps two at a time. As he sat, she grinned at him.

"I overslept," he whispered. "I have this assignment that's giving me fits. I can't seem to concentrate."

"Me, neither."

He set the notebook down on the desktop, and she grabbed it.

I don't know if I can go to church with you this weekend. She looked at him trying to make her best puppy face, pleading.

He reached for the notebook, shaking his head. *Oh, no*! *You promised.*

She looked away, staring at Professor Hartman as if she were listening. He was right. She had promised. Besides, what could it hurt? As long as no one saw her, and it was only the one time.

Aliyah peered back at David, their eyes locked, and she nodded. She read the depth of his compassion in his face. He would never hurt her intentionally. She wrote, *so how long is it again*?

From ten until noon on Sunday.

Shabbat lasts until Saturday evening. I need Sunday to do homework.

Nope. I went with you last weekend. Now it's your turn.

She couldn't think of another objection. There was nothing to be done but go with him.

At lunch, David asked, "So what's so bad about going to my church?"

She put her fork down. "What's the point?"

"You might like it."

He was smiling, but she glared at him. "You believe

in Jesus, or as Jews call him *Yeshu*. You believe in—how do you say—a Father, Son, and Holy Ghost God."

David nodded and finished chewing. "The trinity of God," he confirmed.

Maybe she could help him understand. "But the Torah says in Deuteronomy 6:4, 'Hear O Israel: the Lord our God, the Lord is one!'"

David smiled at her. "So, you're saying you don't believe in a God that is three persons, but only one God. What if I can take your own word, The Tanakh, and show you how this is possible?"

"You can't." She had spent time learning and memorizing the Torah and reading all the books of The Tanakh.

"What about Genesis 1:2 that says, 'the *Spirit* of God was hovering over the face of the waters.'? And what about Genesis 1:26 where God said, 'let us make man in *our* image, after *our* likeness'?"

She knew those verses and had never noticed that wording before, but he was right.

David continued. "And even in Deuteronomy 6:4 where it says, 'God, the Lord is one,' the Hebrew word for 'one' is the same word used in Genesis where God said, 'a man shall leave his father and mother and cleave unto his wife and the two shall be ***one*** flesh.'" David gestured quotes with his fingers when he said ***one***. "Aliyah, the Hebrew word, *Elohim*, is plural not singular."

"David, I'm Jewish. I know the teachings of my religion." She wasn't going to listen to him. What did he know? She had been raised in wisdom.

They both continued eating for an awkward few minutes. Then, David broke the silence. "So, happy anniversary."

Aliyah smiled and gave him a sideward glance. "You remembered." Since they'd never talked before about it being the first day they met, his remembering touched her, and she almost cried.

His hand covered hers. "Eleven years ago today, my bus stopped to pick you up. I was fighting mad cause I couldn't wait to get to school and see Chad."

Aliyah laughed. "What?" She had never known this.

He nodded. "That was until I saw you. Even at seven years old, I knew there was something special about you."

She wriggled her fingers free and wrapped them around his as they stared at each other. That's when he took from his pocket a small box and placed it on the table.

"Don't worry," he quipped. "It's not a ring."

She knew he was referring to her reaction when he gave her the opal ring on her twelfth birthday, but she laughed and said nothing. How it had pained her to give it back that day. What had become of that ring?

She reached in her bag and retrieved her wrapped box.

"What's this?" he asked.

"You're not the only one who has a memory."

He took her gift, and their eyes locked. "Fair enough, but you first."

Aliyah opened the box and gasped. Inside sat a white gold heart with diamonds and diamond earrings for pierced ears. "They're beautiful. I love them." Aliyah put the heart necklace around her neck but didn't say anything about her ears not being pierced. She pushed her wrapped box closer to him. "Your turn."

"What's in here? What did you get me?" He shook it to see if it rattled.

"You'll have to open it to find out."

He tore into the wrapper.

"It's my favorite," she said when he held up the bottle of True Star cologne.

"I still have the last bottle, but it doesn't smell the same as it used to."

They stared at each other, talking with their eyes. Once outside, he put his arm around her. She fingered the heart draped around her neck, and while she loved it, she loved the fact that he remembered more. 9/11, the day of horrible memories for so many, was a day of beginnings for the two of them.

Chapter Fifteen

Sunday morning came without hesitation. Aliyah searched her closet for the right clothes, but she wasn't sure what that might be. David said she could wear anything from jeans to a dress. Should be easy, but nerves caused her to second-guess her every choice.

When David arrived outside, she slipped into her sneakers. Due to the morning chill she chose a long-sleeved, form-fitting t-shirt over her low-rise jeans. She'd pulled her hair into a ponytail and, after a quick glance in the mirror, she headed down the hall, then forced herself to take each step to the truck. The only redeeming thing about this morning was spending time with David. He jumped out and opened her door, one of the few real gentlemen left in the world today. Aliyah felt special whenever he touched her hand, put his arm around her, or softly kissed her goodnight.

David pulled into a parking space outside Faith Family Church, a white building with a tall steeple. They joined the others making their way to the big double doors. As she and David walked inside, people were standing in clusters or sitting on long benches. David led her down the center aisle. Aliyah returned the smiles of people she didn't know. Then, she stared straight at the stage in front. It wasn't the altar that caught Aliyah's attention, but rather the huge wooden cross hanging high in the middle of the wall. She stopped.

David looked at her. He motioned to the left row with his arm. "We can sit right here."

What was she doing here? Why had David insisted she come? He didn't understand.

A man in a suit stood in the aisle and offered his hand. "You must be Aliyah."

"Aliyah, this is Pastor Tom."

She smiled and shook his hand, but she certainly didn't feel any less ill at ease. "It's nice to meet you…Pastor Tom."

David put his arm around her waist. Soon, the band began to play, and everyone stood and sang Awesome God. People raised their hands, some closed their eyes, young and old alike lifted their voices. The words of the song reminded her of passages in the Torah acknowledging God is awesome, wise, and powerful. Aliyah observed those around her. The sights and sounds were beautiful, except for that overbearing cross at the front.

At the end of the song, Pastor Tom prayed. He finished with, "in the name of our Lord Jesus Christ, amen."

They sang more songs, and as Aliyah glanced at those around her, joy showed on their faces, yet Aliyah was conflicted.

Pastor Tom stood when everyone sat. "Today, we're going to talk about ***chosen vessels***. Are you a Chosen Vessel?" He straightened his tie and cleared his throat.

"I'll start reading in Acts Chapter 9." After he read, the pastor told about a man named Saul, almost two thousand years ago. "A respected man," he said, "who was a Roman and a Jew with strong feelings of hatred against Christians. His passion in life was to slaughter them and rid the country of them. Saul was the one who held the clothes of those who stoned Stephen. This man was on his way to Damascus to continue his deadly pursuit of Christians. Along the road, though, something happened."

The pastor's voice became more animated. "A blinding light and a resounding voice spoke to him on that road. And Jesus revealed himself, not by sight, for Saul's eyes had been blinded by the light. Saul cried out, 'Who art thou, Lord?'" Pastor Tom paused. "Jesus answered, 'I am,' which should have been enough, but in case Saul had any doubts, he continued, 'Jesus.' 'I-AM-JESUS.' Saul trembled and asked, 'what would you have me do?'"

Aliyah's own hands trembled. She glanced at that cross and remembered her parents' words years ago when she asked if she could go to church with David's family. *Hitler was a Christian,* they'd shrieked. *Do you want to comingle with Christians?* But even back then she knew David was no Hitler.

Pastor Tom continued, and she fastened her eyes on him. "The Lord told Saul to go into the city. Saul had to be led there because the light had blinded him. In a vision, the Lord told a disciple named Ananias to go to the house of Judas and find Saul. Now, Ananias had heard of this man, Saul, and the bad things he had done toward Christians. 'Lord,' Ananias said, 'are you sure?' But the Lord said unto him, 'go thy way; for he is a chosen vessel unto me, to bear my name before the Gentiles, the kings, and the children of Israel.'"

The pastor paused and his eyes scanned across all those seated, including Aliyah. "So, I ask you again. Are you a chosen vessel?"

Aliyah stole a glance at David whose attention was on the pastor. She quickly looked back, not wanting him to notice. For some reason, her pulse quickened, and she found herself drawn to the words this man spoke.

"Remember what Jesus told us?" Pastor Tom continued. "He said, 'you have not chosen me, but I have chosen you…that whatever you ask of the Father in my name, he may give it to you.'" The preacher closed his Book and walked from behind his stand. "This man, Saul, later renamed Paul, did receive his sight once again and went on to be a CHOSEN VESSEL of the Messiah, teaching and preaching and declaring 'For I am not ashamed of the gospel of Christ: for it is the power of God unto salvation to everyone that believes, to the Jew first, and also to the Greek.'"

The man in the front kept talking and Aliyah was drawn to every word. "So, what about this gospel of Christ? How important is it?" The pastor put his fingertips together and studied the floor a moment. "Many of you know I recently buried my brother. Before he died, I asked him, 'do you remember a time when you gave Jesus your heart and asked him to be your savior?'" Pastor Tom lifted his head and looked from person to person. "My brother answered, 'I don't remember a time, but I believe in God.' I told him, 'Satan believes in God, but he isn't going to be in heaven.'"

Tom paused, and Aliyah felt a vise-like grip on her heart. "And I'll close with this. 'He came unto His own and His own received him not.' My friends, there is no way to heaven except through Jesus, the promised Messiah. 'He is the way, the truth, and the life.'" At his direction, everyone bowed their heads.

Aliyah's heart pounded. She could hear it in her ears and feel it in her chest. Tears rolled down her cheeks. Even with her eyes closed, she still saw that cross. It wouldn't go away. There was light behind it and shooting out from it. For some inexplicable reason, Aliyah couldn't stop crying. She forgot about her objection to the trinity. She forgot about her objection to Jesus. Somehow, she knew within her soul the truth of what she'd heard, but that didn't stop the pastor from speaking.

"That day in his hospital room, my brother bowed his head and asked Jesus to forgive him of his sins. That day, my brother put his faith in Jesus. Is this your day? He became a Chosen Vessel. What say you?"

Aliyah had to make that cross go away. She opened her eyes and lifted her head, but there it was, front and center and bolder than before.

"If you'd like to pray," the pastor's words kept coming. "I invite you to come to the altar. If you need help praying, I'll help you. If you need someone to come with you, nudge the person on your side."

Aliyah had to get out of here.

The music started playing. People around her sang, "Softly and tenderly Jesus is calling." She glanced at David, his head bowed, and his eyes closed. She stood and squeezed in front of him. She intended to leave the pew and race for the back door. As she stepped one foot into the aisle, she could see the door. It seemed to be moving farther away.

A hand grabbed hers, and she turned to see David, his face full of love and concern. Her tears kept falling. Aliyah willed her feet to move and take her out of there, but she froze. David stood and wrapped his arms around her. A voice in her head kept screaming, "no, no, no!"

"Do you want me to go with you?" David asked.

Aliyah stared at him for several seconds, thoughts of her parents and her little sister playing in her mind. She thought about Shabbat and Yom Kippur. Somehow the grace in them became even more perfect in this man Jesus and that cross at the front. She knew David was offering not to take her out the door in the back, but to walk with her forward toward the altar and that cross. She nodded, then whispered, "Yes."

In David's hand, Aliyah found comfort. With each step forward, she felt the pull of that cross like metal to a magnet. The closer she got the lighter she became. Her tears flowed freely, but pure joy made her smile.

Pastor Tom grinned. "Ah, Aliyah. Why have you come?"

David squeezed her hand, and she found her voice. "Jesus," she managed. "I've come because of Jesus." She stared at the cross behind the pastor.

"Do you understand you're a sinner?"

David handed her a tissue from the box on the altar.

"Yes." No one knew this more than she, except for God.

"Jesus came to earth and died to save His people from their sins and was resurrected that we all might live."

She found herself falling in love with this man, Jesus.

"Do you want to put your faith and trust in Him as your savior?"

Aliyah only nodded, but deep down in her soul, she answered a resounding yes.

With her hand in his, Pastor Tom bowed his head and began praying. He told her to repeat after him and she did. With each word a tremendous peace covered her, a feeling like none she'd ever known.

Afterward, she and David sat on the front pew, his arm around her shoulder. She couldn't remember when she'd been this happy if ever.

Chapter Sixteen

"Oh, David." Aliyah wrapped her arm inside his and leaned her head against his shoulder as they drove through the countryside. She couldn't stop laughing. "I feel wonderful."

He grinned. "What do you want to do? Where do you want to go?"

"Anywhere. Let's drive up to the mountaintops, and I'll fly over the valleys below." She looked into his face. "I could, you know. I think I really could."

David laughed. "If I didn't know better, I'd swear you were drunk."

She rested her head back and closed her eyes. Then she opened them wide, "I want to tell somebody. Anybody." She saw a man walking on the sidewalk. "Pull over. I want to tell him." She didn't wait for David's response but slid toward the door, and he abruptly steered the pickup to the side of the road.

"Aliyah, wait," he hollered, but she swung the door open and bounced out.

Rushing to the man, she boldly announced with her arms stretched outward and upward, "I accepted Jesus today." And then she considered the stranger. "Have you accepted Jesus?"

The man moved to the other side of the walk and increased his pace, frowning.

David left the truck and raced around to join Aliyah. "Good morning, Sir. She's a little excited." He wrapped his arm around her waist, preventing her from pursuing her conquest. As the man hurried away, David called out to him, "Have a great day."

"What's wrong with him?" Aliyah stared at David. "He needs to know. The whole world needs to know."

"Well, you're right about that."

Aliyah swung around and stared into the eyes of the one she loved. "Oh, David, thank you." She wrapped her arms around him. "Thank you for taking me to church. Thank you for not letting me change my mind."

He laughed and cupped the side of her face with his palm. He didn't have to say, "I love you" for her to know it. She could stare into his blue eyes forever, but she closed hers as he kissed her. On that sidewalk in broad daylight, with the sound of cars passing, his kiss transported her into a weightless oblivion which sent her soaring above the clouds.

A passing car honked and broke the trance.

"Come on." David pulled her back toward the pickup.

"But, if I don't tell someone, I'm going to burst."

"I have an idea," he said. They climbed in, he pulled out his cell phone and touched it, then handed it to her. "It's Melissa."

Aliyah eagerly accepted. "I haven't talked to her in, " she said as it rang.

"Hey, little brother."

"Uh, no. It's Aliyah."

Melissa's tone became frantic. "Is David okay?"

"Everything's fine." She heard Melissa exhale. "I just had to talk to someone, and he called you."

"Oh. That's nice. Hi."

"I wanted to tell someone that…I accepted Jesus today."

Melissa gasped. "Oh, Aliyah. That's so awesome. Tell me all about it."

~

David listened as Aliyah became animated about her experience. When she hung up, he said, "I would call my parents, but they're in Milan celebrating their anniversary. They'll be thrilled to hear."

The look on Aliyah's face changed to a distant stare. "What? Did I say something wrong?"

She frowned, and stress lines formed on her forehead and around her eyes. She stared at him. "I can never tell my parents. They can never know."

David remembered what his Mom and Dad told him about her having to choose between him and her parents. He pounded the steering wheel with his fist. "Why is that? I don't understand. Christians are good people. How—"

She interrupted. "David…Hitler was a Christian."

Her statement couldn't have sounded more foreign to him. He shook his head and glanced across the street, searching for an answer. "Hitler…was no Christian."

"He proclaimed to be, and that's all my family knows," she mumbled.

David had studied about the Holocaust, he'd even read some books, but like all Christians, the evil actions of that Nazi antichrist and the atrocities he committed turned David's insides out and grieved his soul. He began to understand things from her parents' point of view. "So, when they wouldn't let us be together before, it was because they associated me with Hitler and the terrible things he did?"

She squinted and nodded, "Yes."

"It must have been really hard for you to ask them if I could go to your bat mitzvah."

Aliyah threw her head back and stared at the top of the truck. "It was the hardest thing I ever did, but you had wanted to go so badly."

David squeezed her hand.

Aliyah continued, "I should have known better than to ask them because that made them aware of my feelings for you. During the celebration, they could tell I wasn't happy, even though I pretended. The two of them fought, and Dad decided to move us to Tel Aviv."

David grimaced, fully understanding what his parents were trying to tell him. "Oh, Aliyah. I'm so sorry." He started the ignition and pulled onto the road. They drove in silence, pondering their pathway forward. As she sat beside him, her head resting on his shoulder, he felt grateful despite the obvious difficulties ahead.

During the next weeks, they spent every possible moment together; they studied together either at the library or in his dorm room and they ate lunch together. Thursday evenings became their date night. Aliyah wanted to observe the Sabbath and David understood. They laughed over the silliest things, and the world sparkled anew about them. They hung out sometimes with friends, but for the most part, it was as if they existed together alone.

Whether holding hands, kissing, or staring into her eyes, he felt complete. The happiness he'd lost was found. Just like the two people in their song, "Chasing Cars," they ignored the world, and everything was perfect.

Sunday mornings they worshipped together. When the pastor taught, Aliyah paid complete attention. Sometimes David and she would compare the similarities in the Tanakh and the Bible when they studied their Bible lesson.

The countryside blushed with color, and the weather began to change. Cold winds blew, and with November came the first snowfall. As the temperature dropped, David's love kept him warm. They threw snowballs at each other and made snow angels. In their spare time, they visited the shops downtown and picked up gifts for loved ones.

"So, why don't you come home with me for Thanksgiving?" David asked while Aliyah perused music boxes for her little sister. "Melissa will be there and even Scott is supposed to make an appearance sometime during the break."

She inhaled and sighed. "I'm supposed to go to my Uncle's."

David's hope dissipated. "I guess you have to." The thought of Aliyah spending Thanksgiving with him and his family thrilled him, but he understood. Her parents probably received updates from her aunt and uncle.

~

Aliyah picked up the snow globe, the one with the Christmas tree, snowman, and snow. She wanted to share with her little sister about the true meaning of Christmas. She'd thought about purchasing the globe with the nativity and even the one with Bethlehem and the star, but the time wasn't right yet.

As they walked hand in hand toward campus, Aliyah couldn't stop thinking about David's suggestion. Oh, how she wanted to go with him. How she didn't want to go to her Uncle's. She chose courage over wisdom and announced, "Yes, I will go with you at Thanksgiving. I'll call my aunt and tell her I've made other plans. I'm eighteen now, so I can make my own decisions."

"I don't know, Aliyah. Are you sure?"

Her heart leapt with joy at her plan. "Yes." She laughed. "I'm sure."

~

After the final class dismissed before Thanksgiving break, Aliyah rushed back to her dorm, changed clothes, and threw her toiletries into her suitcase before zipping it up.

Her phone chimed with a message from David. *Are you ready? I'll be there in ten minutes.*

Her hands trembled as she responded, *yes*. Aliyah's aunt objected when she told her she'd made other plans, but Aliyah refused to let it ruin her time. When David pulled up outside, she dashed out the door.

During the four-and-a-half-hour drive, they talked and listened to music. She enjoyed being close to him, feeling their legs touching, resting her head on his shoulder, entwining their fingers.

"What if your parents don't like me?" Aliyah asked as nerves surfaced about meeting them. "What if they don't understand about us?"

"Not a chance. Besides, they're a bit like us."

"What do you mean?"

"They came from two different worlds, too. My mom's dad was a factory worker, but my dad's dad is a multi-billionaire."

"How did they end up together?"

"It's an interesting story."

"Tell me."

"My dad deceived my mom, and as a result, she ran away, gave birth to Melissa, and then gave her up for adoption."

"What?" Aliyah's eyes were saucers.

"Yeah, it was a twist of fate that brought them back together."

When David pulled into the drive of his home, her hands trembled.

"David," his mom exclaimed, as she greeted him at the back door with a kiss. "And this must be Aliyah. My, how beautiful you've become." She hugged her, making Aliyah feel welcome but awkward at the same time.

"Thank you for having me, Mrs. Drake."

"Please call me, Beth."

David's mom's glowed with a natural beauty, and their home was nothing like Aliyah expected. She'd feared it might be cold and formal, but the den and the kitchen were warm and cozy with harvest decorations and pumpkins and the scent of cinnamon and apples.

David barely said hello to his mother. "Is Mel here?"

"Yep. She's upstairs in her room."

David grabbed Aliyah's hand. "Come on. We'll go surprise her." And with that, he pulled her down the hall, into the foyer, and up the stairs.

Melissa hugged Aliyah, and the three of them sat in her room and chatted about school, Melissa's new boyfriend, and what they wanted to do while home.

Aliyah hadn't met David's dad except for having seen him at a school play one year. She really didn't remember what he looked like.

That evening, as they gathered in the dining room, Mr. Drake entered and introduced himself. "Aliyah." He held out his hand. "David's told us so much about you." An attractive man for his age, Mr. Drake was an older image of David. His handshake ended in him pulling her into a fatherly hug.

"He talks about the two of you a lot, also."

The family sat around the table and Mr. Drake prayed like David always did before the two of them ate. He ended with, "in the name of Jesus Christ, Amen." Aliyah felt a kindred spirit here. There was a peace in this home.

"I understand that the two of you traveled to Milan recently," Aliyah said while passing the asparagus.

"Yeah, don't forget. I want to see pictures," David added.

Beth passed potatoes. "We don't want to bore you guys with pictures."

Mr. Drake talked about them also going to Paris.

"Oh, my goodness," Aliyah exclaimed. "I've always wanted to go to Paris. I want to walk down whatever that street is with the Eiffel Tower lit up in the distance while listening to '*La Vie en Rose*.'"

"Yes." Beth's face beamed. "We did that." She touched Mr. Drake's hand. "It is definitely the city of love."

Aliyah admired David's parents and wished hers were more like them.

"M-o-m," Melissa dragged the name out, "we gotta see pictures."

"Maybe later this week. We want to spend time with you kids and get to know Aliyah."

That evening, the five of them played games in the den. Later, Beth showed Aliyah to her room.

Thanksgiving Day arrived. Melissa and Aliyah helped Beth with the turkey while David and his dad ran an errand. Grandma and Grandpa Brown arrived from Hartford, and the house buzzed with activity and joy. Once again, they prayed before the Thanksgiving meal, but this time each one around the table expressed gratitude for at least one thing.

Mr. and Mrs. Drake were thankful to have their family home. "And, especially, to have you with us, Aliyah," Beth added.

Everyone made her feel special, and David turned to her when it was his time. "I'm thankful for God's hand of fate." He kissed her lightly.

Aliyah lifted her glass. "And I'm thankful for government class." Those who knew the story laughed.

"What class?" Grandma Brown asked.

"Government class." Melissa explained how that mix-up allowed David and Aliyah to find each other again.

Grandpa Brown summed it up. "God works in mysterious ways."

~

Saturday evening, Mr. Drake brought in the cut Christmas tree and David carried the pine garland. Beth came down the stairs with a box in her arms.

"Mom." David jumped up to take it from her. "I'll get the Christmas decorations out of the attic."

"I'll let you and your father get the rest of them."

Melissa busied herself with the garland and ribbons.

"What can I do?" Aliyah asked.

"Help us decorate the tree," Beth exclaimed.

Aliyah enjoyed looking at the ornaments. It seemed there was a story behind each one, especially the homemade ones. She loved David's family. That evening, his mom made hot cocoa, and they sat by the fire and watched home videos. There was film of school programs and one in particular of her and David in the second grade. They all laughed and told stories, some of them unknown to the others, like David explaining how his teal tie and magenta shirt were to match Aliyah's colors that night of the dance.

In the midst of the merriment, Aliyah's phone buzzed, and she saw a missed call from her mother. Should she ignore it? Her parents never called. No, she'd have to call back. Her pulse increased at the thought.

"What's wrong?" David questioned.

She showed him her phone, and their eyes locked. "I'll have to go somewhere and call home."

"We can call from my truck."

"I need to be alone."

He clasped her hand in his and dug his keys out of his pocket. "Here, you can start it up and run the heater while you talk."

Aliyah took them gratefully. In a few minutes, she slipped through the garage and out to his truck. She started it and turned up the heater. The joy of this day morphed into a sense of foreboding. She imagined a make-believe clock striking midnight. With the phone to her ear, she waited for her world to fall apart.

Chapter Seventeen

David noticed Aliyah's mood changed after the call. Several times he asked how it went, but her noncommittal response was always, "it was fine." During their quiet drive back to Ithaca, she rested her head against his shoulder, but the laughter disappeared.

When he purposefully put in their CD and the music played, she didn't sing. Instead, a tear rolled down her cheek before she wiped it away. Hard as he tried, she refused to talk.

David parked outside her dorm and turned the ignition off. He held her tight and didn't want to let go. When he kissed her, she clung to him and he found it difficult to stop. In the moonlight, he felt the softness of her cheek and saw the longing in her eyes. He kissed her face all over before moving to her ear lobes and exploring the softness of her neck. He needed her for she was like the air to him. "Oh, Aliyah," he whispered in her ear. "I love you. Marry me. Marry me now." He pulled away to see her reaction. Her eyes were filled with tears. "What? What is it? What happened when you talked to your parents?"

She grimaced, then started to sob. "I have to go." She scooted to the door and opened it.

"Aliyah, wait." David bound out of the truck and rushed around the front of it, but she'd already raced down the walk and disappeared behind the closing door. "Your bag," he yelled.

He texted her as he returned to the truck. *You need your bag. Please tell me what's wrong.*

His phone chimed. *I love you. DAVE. With all my heart.*

Her text put his mind at ease a bit. He wanted to believe her reaction was because she thought he went too far. He wanted to believe that *DAVE* was as light-hearted as their other teasing. But there was something familiar in her tears, something familiar in the despair of her face. Still, he texted back: *All of me loves you. And it's DAVID!*

Sleep was slow in coming, and when it did, it came in the form of a nightmare; Aliyah standing at the rail of a ship, her arms outstretched to him as he stood on shore, watching the ship disappear into the mist of the sea.

When David awoke, he ached to see her, but she had an early morning class on Mondays. In fact, it was a full day for her. He'd text later and ask what she wanted him to do with her bag.

Aliyah failed to text or show up at lunch. He usually didn't hear from her on the first day of the week until evening, and then it was just in the form of a text. There wasn't enough time for her to cross campus and make it back again before her next class.

It was about four in the afternoon when David decided to send a message. *Hey, beautiful. Hope you're having a great day. Want me to bring your bag over?*

Aliyah wouldn't be free from her last class until about five. David worked on an assignment for sociology and didn't look up until his stomach growled at six. He checked his messages but nothing from her. She could be busy working on assignments or studying for final exams. Her math class had been giving her trouble. Still, how long did it take to answer a simple text?

At seven o'clock, David decided to drive by her dorm and at least deliver her bag. He was hoping he could talk her into dinner. Surely, she had time to eat. He walked down the hall and up the stairs, avoiding students coming and going. On the second floor, the door to Aliyah's room was halfway open. Her roommate was talking with someone. He assumed it was Aliyah until he saw her face and realized her hair was lighter and shorter.

"You looking for Aliyah?" her roommate asked.

"Yeah, have you seen her?"

"Not this evening, but when she left this morning, she said she'd be late. Something about math tutoring."

David nodded. "I'll go ahead and leave this, then." He set her bag on the floor next to her bed. "She might need it." Once out in the hall, he wondered if he should wait, but he had his own work to finish.

Now he knew what was keeping her. She'd told him last week she'd called a tutor. He was glad she connected with someone who could help, but he hated having to wait until government class tomorrow to see her. Maybe she'd call when she finished. What if the tutor was a guy—maybe even Michael—and she decided to have dinner with him? Jealousy stung him, but he dismissed it as easily as it came.

It was another night of restless sleep for David. Aliyah didn't return his texts. Had he done something to offend her? He had wanted her that night, but he stopped. Never would he take advantage of her. He loved her too much. It was four in the morning the last time he looked at his phone and he hadn't really been to sleep. Any time he drifted off, he stood on the shore again, watching her leave. He ran through the sand barefoot to swim toward the ship. Before he made it to the water, bullets riddled his body. Pain pierced his heart and he fell face-first into the water.

He gasped and bolted up in bed. It was light outside, too light. He grabbed his phone—nine-forty-seven. He jumped out of bed, checked his messages, and still nothing. He threw on some clothes, brushed his teeth, swung one strap of his backpack over his shoulder, and put his shoes on as he rushed out the door. There wasn't time to shower or shave. Come to think of it, he'd forgotten to shave yesterday, too.

David raced to McGraw Hall and rushed into class ten seconds before it started. He took the steps two at a time, but when he glanced at their usual spot, she wasn't there. Professor Hartman began talking about the state of the nation after the re-election of President Obama. It was no secret he approved. David stared at the door, expecting to see her any moment, knowing that Hartman wouldn't like it if she were late.

Fifteen minutes passed and David became more and more uneasy. His mind raced. The last time she texted him was Sunday evening. He hadn't heard from her at all yesterday, but her roommate said she was there Monday morning. Did she come home last night? He risked the wrath of Hartman and sent her another text. *Where are you? Prof H is talking socialism again.*

David wrapped, unwrapped, and wrapped again the

string from his hoodie around his finger, willing his phone to action. His heart pounded in his ears. The hair on his neck stood up. Minutes ebbed in slow motion. Ten minutes passed and still nothing.

That was it! He grabbed his jacket and backpack and slipped past the other students taking notes of Professor Hartman's lecture. As David hurried down the stairs, Professor H stopped his diatribe and called his name.

"Did someone sound the fire alarm, Mr. Drake?" Some of the students laughed.

David's face warmed, and he didn't mean to be disrespectful, but he just couldn't stop, so he pushed through the door and out of the building. He ran all the way to Aliyah's dorm. As he reached the second floor, his breath came in gasps. David knocked on her door. Nothing. He knocked again. Finally, he decided to try the knob. It was unlocked. He walked inside.

Neither Aliyah nor her roommate were there. Aliyah's bed didn't look slept in, but she could've made it before leaving. Her suitcase sat on the floor in the same spot where he had left it and a pair of socks remained untouched on the rug. David panicked. Frantically, he looked inside the closet. Her clothes were there.

David called her again. Her phone rang three times before going to voicemail. "Hi. You've reached Aliyah. I'm not here…well, I am here. I just can't talk right now, so leave a message. *Shalom*."

After the beep, he decided to do just that. "Aliyah, are you alright? You haven't returned any of my texts. I'm worried. Please call, okay?"

David was back where he'd begun, waiting for Aliyah to call or text. Worry overwhelmed him. Something wasn't right. As he was leaving, a girl entered and started up the stairs.

"Have you seen Aliyah from 208?" he asked.

"No, I haven't seen her today."

"Did you see her yesterday?"

"I don't think I've seen her since Thanksgiving break."

David took a deep breath. His frustration was getting the better of him. He wanted to kick something. But what he really wanted was to hear Aliyah's voice.

God, I pray you'd let me know about her. Protect her from harm. Why hadn't he prayed before now? He believed in God. Why did he rely on himself in times of trouble instead of asking for help? He remembered praying as a twelve-year-old that Aliyah wouldn't leave, but her family took her away anyway.

David headed to the Jewish Center. Maybe someone there might know something. A woman at the center said she hadn't seen her since before break. He waited around outside the center for two hours, forgetting all about his next class. The wind blew hard and cold, and David pulled his hood over his head.

Just as he was leaving, he spied Michael some fifty yards away. He ran to him. "Hey, Michael, right?"

"That's right. And you're Aliyah's boyfriend?"

"Yeah. Have you seen her?"

"I saw her in class yesterday morning. Why?"

David took a deep breath, thankful to have found someone else who had interacted with her recently. "Have you seen her at all today?"

Michael wrinkled his eyebrows. "No. What's going on?"

"She's not returning my texts or answering my calls. I'm looking for anyone who's seen her."

Michael's eyes darted from right to left and he rubbed his chin. "Look, I don't know if I should say anything, but she said that her parents weren't happy with her."

David had almost forgotten about the call to her parents. "What did she tell you?"

"Not much. Just that she was supposed to go to her uncle's over the break. She was afraid they might pull her back home."

"What?" David practically shrieked. "Before the end of the semester? That's crazy." David started pacing and ran his hands through his hair.

"Not really, Dude. Not with a religious family like hers. She is to honor her father and mother."

David shook his head with numerous questions running through his mind. Why didn't she tell him? Then he asked, "Could they have come and taken her home before she could call me?"

Michael smirked. "Oh yeah. But that's not the worst. In Israel they didn't allow her access to the internet. They may have taken her cell phone."

David shook his head. "Who does that? I don't understand. Why?"

"Look, I don't know if they know, but she told me she'd converted to Christianity. If they find out…" His voice trailed off.

"What will happen if they found out?" David shouted.

"It won't be good."

David stared into a smoky gray sky and took a deep breath, panic seizing his heart. "Thanks, man." He took his cell out of his coat pocket. "Can I have your number? If I find out something, I'll call you, and maybe you can do the same?"

They quickly exchanged numbers. He might need Michael. In their short conversation, he learned Aliyah had divulged more to Michael than she'd shared with him. And Michael understood her situation better than he did.

It was now four o'clock. If David hurried, he might make it to the dean's office before they closed. He ran all the way. Of all the days not to have his truck but finding parking during the week on campus was always difficult.

Mr. Hudspeth, the dean, was still in his office and reluctantly agreed to meet with David, despite his lack of an appointment. This balding man in his late forties finally looked up from his desk, even though David had been seated in the chair right in front of him for what seemed like an eternity. "Now, Mr. Drake, how can I help you?"

"It's about another student, Aliyah Zimmerman. I believe she may be missing, and I'm not sure how to go about reporting it."

"And what makes you think this?"

David relayed his attempts to reach her the last two days. As he talked, he explored the foul-play scenario and became terrified. He stood. "I'm sorry, Dean Hudspeth. I realize I should go straight to the police." He whipped around and stepped toward the door.

Dean Hudspeth cleared his throat. "Come back, Mr. Drake, please." David turned and the dean motioned to the chair. "Come. Please, sit back down."

David hesitated but finally complied.

"Miss Zimmerman's uncle, a Mr. Levi Zimmerman, withdrew her yesterday morning at the request of her parents. I assure you she's fine. Her family needed her to return home."

David's mouth dropped. Surely, it couldn't be this easy. "She's not fine. They're withdrawing her against her will."

"They are her parents. We cannot keep her here. Besides, she's an Israeli citizen."

Never had four words made a bigger impact in David's life. Sharper than any knife, they pierced his heart. The wide expanse between their two worlds had separated them once again. David stared at Dean Hudspeth, at a loss for words.

No, God! He arose and strode out of the office in shock. He trudged back to his dorm, climbed in his truck, and drove to the botanic gardens.

The guard yelled at him that they would be closing soon, but he ignored him. He was on a mission to reach the spot where he and Aliyah had gazed up at a colorful sky. David remembered telling her it was made for them. But now, dark clouds of the impending winter's storm replaced the purple and red hues of their sky. With all the frustration pent up inside him, he yelled, "Why, God?"

Tears formed and he couldn't prevent them. That's when he heard it, ever so soft, perhaps only a whisper in his ear. *Go After Her*.

He wiped at the wetness on his face. Once again, he looked upward. "Okay, but you go with me."

Chapter Eighteen

As David got back behind the wheel, his thoughts raced. What was the matter with him? How little he knew about Aliyah and her family. He didn't even know her parents' first names. They lived in Tel Aviv, but he didn't have the address, the phone number, not anything. How was he going to find out what happened to her? He needed to go to New York and see if he could find her Aunt and Uncle, Levi Zimmerman. Maybe Aliyah was with them. He knew if he left, he'd jeopardize his grades. He thought about Aliyah and how hard she had worked at her classes. All for nothing. His heart ached to hold her.

When David returned to his dorm, music blared from one of the rooms. The next house was having a party. David ignored everyone. He sat on his bed and made notes of everything he could remember. Zimmerman, Tel-Aviv, little sister, an all-girls school…He didn't have much to go on.

Then a new idea occurred to him—he needed to call Aunt BJ. She was a private investigator. Maybe she could locate Aliyah or her relatives.

Even though it was cold, David stepped outside

where it was quieter.

"Hi, David," BJ answered.

"Aunt BJ, I need your help." David had no time for small talk. Instead, he relayed his story to BJ and all he knew about Aliyah.

"Let me check around and see what I can find. You take care of your classes and let me do this," she instructed him. "I'll call you tomorrow evening and let you know what I find out."

"Thanks, Aunt BJ. But still, it's going to be hard for me to be productive here at school."

"I know, but you hang in there. You only have, what, maybe two weeks?"

When David hung up, he knew the next two weeks would be the longest days of his life. How in the world was he going to complete assignments, much less study for exams?

That night, he awoke every two hours, his mind filled with worry for Aliyah. He had to remind himself to pray and trust, but it didn't come easily. In the morning, he dressed and brushed his teeth, but he hadn't shaved for three consecutive days and looked a little scruffy when he left for his morning class.

He turned in some assignments but wasn't sure if they contained coherent thoughts. David went through the motions of his regular Wednesday routine, eager for evening to arrive and to hear what BJ had to tell him. Finally, she called.

"I checked with the registrar's office and tracked down Aliyah's Aunt and Uncle here in the city."

"Yes?" David's heart pounded. *Please tell me good news*.

"She's not here."

David's heart sank.

"Her parents flew her back to Israel," BJ continued.

David chucked his book across the room. "I've got to go after her."

"David, listen to me," BJ reasoned. "You need to finish the semester—"

"No. I need to be on a plane to Tel Aviv as soon as possible."

"And we'll get you to Tel Aviv, but first let me put a plan together, and—"

"What plan?" All he could think about was her parents' possible retribution for her conversion, or a forced early marriage to Jacob Steiner.

"Let me put you a team together first. You can't just go over there without support. There's a company. It's owned by two former Israeli intelligence officers. We worked together with Scotland Yard on another case."

BJ made a lot of sense and he understood the wisdom in it. "Okay, you get it together and I'll be on the first plane after that."

"Stay put, David. Continue your classes until the end of the semester. In the meantime, I'll lay the groundwork, and we'll have a plan in place by the time you get there."

~

In the last two weeks, David found it difficult to breathe. He tried to do classwork and study for exams, but truth be known, he had no idea if he'd passed any of them, nor did he care.

The cab stopped in front of the United Airlines terminal at JFK International Airport with the snow swirling around it. David grabbed his bag, paid the driver, and climbed out. Cold wind slapped his face and neck, despite his newly acquired beard by default. Even though he wore a heavy coat and scarf, he welcomed the terminal's warmth when he entered through the automatic doors, stomped his feet, and brushed the snow flurries from his arms. A Christmas tree sat in the middle of the two-way escalator and carols played on the speakers.

David retrieved his passport and boarding pass from the inside pocket of his jacket. He continued to the security line. He'd arrived three hours early, giving himself plenty of time. What else did he have to do except sit and dwell on how much he missed Aliyah?

Many times, he'd tried to call her. He never expected her to answer, knowing full well her parents had probably confiscated her phone, but hearing her voice and imagining her smile while she recorded her greeting made him feel closer. "Hi. You've reached Aliyah. I'm not here…well, I am here. I just can't talk right now, so leave a message. Shalom."

"Belgium Airlines flight 1137 to Paris now boarding at gate fifty-nine. Belgium Airlines flight 1137 gate fifty-nine."

The airport had set up additional wait lanes because of the holidays. He sighed. As long as he didn't miss his plane, he'd be alright. It was a twelve-hour flight to Tel Aviv. He traveled coach because all first-class seats were taken. It was the first plane scheduled after he arrived in New York City and God knew he would sit upright for twenty-four hours straight if it would bring him closer to his love.

Waiting at the gate, anxious for them to start boarding and take off, David couldn't sit still. Finally, the agent called for priority boarders, and he was like a horse jumping out of the gate at the starting bell, landing him first in line, as if the plane would get there faster the sooner he boarded.

David walked down the aisle, placed his bag in the overhead bin, and sat next to the window. As others boarded, David put his earbuds in, and the music played. He leaned his head back and closed his eyes. In his memory he lay next to Aliyah in the grass at the botanic gardens, listening to the falls and staring at the sky. He could see her face glowing, her eyes beaming. How he yearned to touch her. Visions of that morning after church came back. In her excitement, she had jumped out of the truck and pursued the man on the sidewalk. David's heart ached. Then, his eyes flew open as he remembered the horror in her eyes when she proclaimed, "I can never tell my parents. They can never find out."

David sat for twelve torturous hours in the air, waiting to arrive. When they disembarked in Tel Aviv, he found himself herded with the crowd to baggage claim. The huge crowd pressed in, eager to be on their way. He saw many signs written in English, Arabic, and Hebrew, which looked like hieroglyphics, Welcome to Israel, Passport Control, and baggage claim.

He waited in a long line to pass through the turnstile toward baggage. When he tried to pass through, it wouldn't budge, and an alarm sounded. A flurry of security guards in uniforms, badges, and firearms yelled at him. At first, he didn't understand what he'd done wrong. Then he figured out he'd missed a step and returned to the passport control line. After waiting almost an hour, it was his turn. He slipped his passport and ID under the glass to the attendant in the booth.

She surveilled him from head to toe. "Mr. Drake,

what are you doing here in Israel?"

BJ had coached him before he left. "I'm here to join a tour group," he answered.

The guard studied him. "Which tour group?"

David's heart pounded, but he remained calm. "Adventure tours."

After a second, the guard shifted into action, punching keys on the computer. In a moment, the printer shot out a card and a ticket. "Keep your visa with you at all times. Use the ticket at the turnstile." She then dismissed David with a single hand motion.

Once David made it through that process, he headed to the exit. He glanced around, looking for the contact person BJ said would meet him. With David's dark brown hair and dark beard, he looked like he belonged, except for his US Olympics T-shirt. He watched everyone. Most were dressed normal, although some men wore long black coats, tall black hats, with beards and long locks of hair on each side. He had seen similar dress in New York City.

Directly ahead, holding a handprinted sign that read *David Drake* was a man in his forties, of medium build and average height.

"I'm David Drake."

The gentleman lowered the sign and offered his hand. "Hello, David, I'm Aharon Levarko."

David raised his brows when Aharon spoke in a distinctive kiwi accent.

"Ah, my accent surprises you. I'm Israeli, but New Zealand born. My mother is actually English." He dropped the sign in a trash bin and motioned to the door. "Right this way. I have a car waiting for us." Aharon raised his arm, and a black sedan pulled up. David followed his lead as the two of them climbed into the back.

"I have a room for you at the Dan Hotel. We'll get up early in the morning and take you shopping."

"Excuse me?" Did this New Zealander believe David had brought a suitcase that contained no clothes?

Aharon glanced at the t-shirt beneath David's coat. "Whatever you may have brought, you're going to need a few minor adjustments. Although I must say, the beard is a nice touch."

David was anxious and tired of waiting. "Have you found the Zimmermans? Have you seen Aliyah?"

"Slow down, mate. There's a bit more to it than that."

"No there isn't." David's impatience surfaced when it seldom ever did. "Hey, I've just traveled by pickup, cab, and plane a total of twenty hours. I appreciate and need your help, but please just give me a straight story. What have you found out?"

Aharon remained unmoved. He lifted his eyes and stared at David with a stone-cold face. "All right. The Zimmermans are no longer in Tel Aviv, Mr. Drake."

It was as if this Israeli punched David in the stomach with his words, wielding his New Zealand kiwi accent, striking him in the center of his heart. David shook his head. "Why? Where did they go?"

Aharon took a deep breath and blew it out slowly. "We're confirming it now, but we believe they've moved to Tiberias on the Sea of Galilee. There, Aliyah is going through a purification time."

David stared at him and felt the canyon dividing him and Aliyah doubling in size. "So, what are we shopping for?"

"With just a few changes in your garments, I think

we can get you an audience with her father."

David's eyes widened and his pulse increased. He turned and stared out the window at storefronts with names written in Hebrew. "I apologize, Mr. Levarko. I realize I'm completely out of my element here, and you're only trying to help me."

"Well, then, David, you can call me Aharon."

The man's cell phone rang. "Shalom." He remained quiet for several seconds, listening. "I see. Text me that, please." When he hung up, he told David, "We've obtained an address in Tiberias." The sedan pulled in front of the hotel and stopped. "We'll get you checked in here, and tomorrow after shopping, we'll begin our journey."

Promptly at eight o'clock in the morning, the black sedan parked outside the lobby. Aharon had their schedule planned. First, a stop at a local store of traditional Israeli clothing.

"I don't understand why I need different clothes." This had confused David from the beginning since his church didn't judge people from the outward appearance.

Aharon handed him a black Yarmulke before moving to white shirts.

"I know what this is for, although I don't get it."

Aharon thumbed through a shirt rack. "You want the girl, right?"

"Yes. But—"

"And you want her parents' blessing?"

"Yes. Is that possible?" David's spirits lifted. Could there be a way to rescue Aliyah and not alienate her family?

"Probably not, but we're going to do our best. What size shirt do you wear?" The Israeli New Zealander surveyed him from his shoulders down to his waist. "Fifteen or sixteen with longer sleeves?"

"Maybe I'm a fifteen with thirty-four-inch sleeves."

Aharon held up a white shirt in front of David. "You should try it on."

"I'm not wearing that."

Mr. Levarko pushed the garment into David's chest and pointed to a fitting room. David sighed and obeyed. When he came out carrying the shirt, Aharon handed him a pair of pants and a jacket.

"Okay, but explain this to me," David demanded. "I'm looking at you and you're dressed pretty normal."

"Yes. Well, I'm a Messianic Jew. And even among us, there are varying levels of observance."

"But why do I need to wear this? Are you telling me Aliyah's family are Orthodox Jews?"

As if Aharon couldn't believe David's ignorance, he nodded thoughtfully before shaking his head. "Not Orthodox like the Hasidic Jews in New York City of whom you might be aware. Aliyah's family is a little more progressive but definitely more than conservative. For example, you don't wear a garment made of wool and linen."

"But why?" All of this seemed so petty to David.

"In Leviticus 19:19 in the Torah, it says not to wear a garment of wool and linen—it has to do with separation, not mixing. It's just that simple."

David squinted his eyes and pursed his lips. "Is this all I need or is there more?" he asked while taking possession of the clothes.

"No, that's it."

David headed to the cash register and pulled out a credit card. He saw a stack of broad-brimmed tall black hats. “You sure I don’t need one of these?”

“I’m sure. Now, you’re just making fun.”

David noticed the corners of Aharon’s mouth curve up slightly at his humor.

Soon, they were on the highway, driving by the Mediterranean Sea and signs that read Caesarea. Then, they turned inland toward Bethsaida and Tiberias on the Sea of Galilee. The journey had taken about two hours when the car parked in front of the Ron Beach Hotel.

“There’s a room reservation here for you. Get checked in, grab a bite, clean up, and put on your new clothes.”

“You’re kidding, right? The ones we just bought?”

“That’s right. I’m going to check out this address and I’ll be back.”

David had started to climb out of the car, but as soon as Aharon mentioned where he was going, David sat back down. “The Zimmermans’? I’m going with you, then.”

Aharon placed his hand on David’s arm. “No, David. Trust me. First, the clothes. Get some rest and I’ll be back. Tonight, is the beginning of Shabbat.”

David couldn’t believe he was this close, and yet he still must wait. “So, are you saying I’m going to wait until Sunday because of Shabbat?”

“No, I’m saying let me confirm things.”

David stared long and hard at Aharon. He felt frustrated and desperate, yet he didn’t want to alienate the only person he knew in Israel, so he followed orders.

Chapter Nineteen

His room overlooked the Sea of Galilee. At four in the afternoon, David stood in front of the mirror and finished buttoning his shirt. After putting the jacket on, he stroked his beard. He realized that with the color of his hair, the fact he hadn't cut it recently and had stopped shaving, he looked like he could've been born here.

David stuck the yarmulke in his pocket and entered the elevator. He felt like an imposter in his new clothes.

When the door opened, Aharon stood waiting. "Oh, good. You got on the right elevator. I forgot to tell you not to take the Shabbat elevator. It stops on all the floors."

David didn't understand. "Why?"

"A Jew is forbidden to work on Shabbat, or the Sabbath. Even pushing buttons for varying floors is considered work. So, the Shabbat elevator stops on all of them."

David blinked hard and realized he had a lot to learn if pushing buttons on an elevator was work. When they walked outside, the temperature had cooled considerably. "Where's the car?" he asked.

"There is no driving on Shabbat, which is starting—" Aharon looked up at the setting sun, "—soon."

David fell into step beside him. "So, where are we going?"

"You've been invited to Shabbat dinner at the Cohens'. They are a religious family. All they know about you is that you're David and you're here from New York. They'll assume you're Jewish."

David stopped, his eyes wide. "You think I can pull that off?"

Aharon smirked and shrugged his shoulders. "We'll see. Depends on how smart you are." He continued walking, leaving David standing there.

David looked toward the sky. *You said you'd go with me*. Then he jogged to catch up.

"When I point the house out to you, you'll knock. When they answer, introduce yourself. Be sure and kiss the *mezuzah* on the doorpost before you enter, like this…" He touched an imaginary mezuzah in the air with two of his fingers and then kissed them.

David nodded.

"Now, do you know anything about a Shabbat dinner?"

"Only a little. I went to one on campus with Aliyah."

Aharon pulled David into an alley. He handed him a sheet of paper with the blessings and song lyrics on it. "How long will it take you to memorize this?"

"This is in Hebrew."

The Israeli thought for a moment. "You'll have to fake your way through it." He took off again and David ran after him.

"Easy for you to say. Won't their normal conversation be in Hebrew?"

"Actually, no. This family was born in America, and they're aware that you don't know the language, so they'll talk in English."

"I don't know about this." David already dreaded the evening.

Once they left the town of Tiberias with its shops and boat docks, they started walking up a hill. The homes on either side were all the same light color. "How much further?" David asked.

"Oh, just about a mile or so up this hill."

Either Aharon walked really fast or David had subconsciously slowed down. He had just increased his pace when his guide stopped.

"That's it straight ahead there."

The house in front of David was like the rest. Inside the courtyard above the block fence, he could make out a woman hurriedly removing laundry from a clothesline.

"I have to leave you here." Aharon pointed to the corner a block down the hill behind them. "I'll wait for you there."

David's stomach flipped. "What? You're not going with me?"

"No. I managed to get you the invitation. The rest is up to you."

David shook his head. "I'm not ready."

"You'll be fine. My daughter is there. Her name is Anna. She'll help you." Aharon looked at the diminishing light in the sky. "Now go on. You don't want to be late."

David drew a deep breath and continued alone. *Lord, I need you now.*

Aharon whistled and David turned around. The Israeli pointed to his own head and David could hardly hear, but he understood. He pulled the yarmulke out of his pocket and placed it on his head.

Upon reaching the door, David knocked. A man in his forties answered.

"Mr. Cohen?" David dipped his head. "*Shabbat Shalom*."

The older man's smile could barely be seen beneath his beard. "Ah, you must be David. Shabbat Shalom. Welcome to my home." He motioned for him to enter.

As David crossed the threshold, he kissed the mezuzah as he'd been shown. Simple furniture, complemented by brilliantly colored and intricately woven rugs and tapestries, filled the dimly lit house, and an unknown spicy fragrance filled the air.

"This is my wife," Mr. Cohen touched the arm of the woman beside him, "Tamara, and you may call me Samuel." Her face lit up when she smiled, and her brown eyes gleamed with flakes of green. She was the one removing the laundry from the line.

"Shabbat Shalom. Thank you for having me, Mrs. Cohen."

Two boys, one about the age of ten and the other a couple of years younger, tried to fit through the doorway simultaneously. It appeared they'd raced to see who could be first. Mr. Cohen scolded them, and immediately their chatter stopped. Each wore black pants with white shirts and black yarmulkes. "These are my sons, Dan and Jonathan."

"Shabbat Shalom," they said in unison.

A slight chuckle escaped David's lips as he replied.

Two young ladies entered from the kitchen. David recognized one as Anna for he could easily see her resemblance to Aharon, and the other looked like

Tamara.

Mr. Cohen continued with the introductions. "And this is my daughter, Rachael, and her new friend, Anna." Without allowing David to do more than smile, his host continued, "and now we should begin the candle lighting."

Rachael bowed modestly and proceeded to an intricately carved, wooden table where candles and a gold-trimmed box sat on a stand covered in fine purple silk. To the side sat the kiddush cup. She placed shekels in the opening of the box.

Anna discreetly moved closer to David as the whole family gathered around. Rachael struck a match and lit both candles. She waved her hands gracefully three times and then placed them over her eyes. Softly, she began singing the blessing of Shabbat.

Barach atah, Adonai Eloheinu, Melech haolam, Asher Kidshanu B'mitzvotav Vitzivanu L'hadlik Ner Shel Shabbat…

Everyone listened and afterward, they said in unison, "Amen."

She then took the kiddush cup and offered what David thought was the same blessing, except for a few words. Toward the end, the family joined in. Anna sang loud, allowing him to lip sync. Then came the ceremonial handwashing before the breaking of bread and the meal.

The Cohen family spoke English and made him feel welcome. Mrs. Cohen's cooking tasted delicious and David enjoyed the food. Dan and Jonathan made him laugh with their antics and the night was off to a good start.

"David, I understand you are here studying our

methods of agriculture," Mr. Cohen said.

David choked on his water and glanced at Anna who sat across from him. He cleared his throat and dabbed at his mouth with his napkin. "That's right. I'm studying several different things in school. Trying to figure out which direction I should go." *Seriously, Aharon. Agriculture? Of all the things you could've chosen, I know the least about agriculture.* "My father thought it would be a good idea to come to the homeland over my break."

"Where are you staying while you're here?" Anna asked.

David was thankful she had changed the subject. "I'm currently at the Ron Beach Hotel."

After dinner, Samuel sat with David in the courtyard. "So, what do you think of Israel? I mean, your father must have thought it was important for you to visit the land of your ancestors."

"Yes, I suppose he did. It is a blessed land and it flows with abundance."

"It does indeed. But do you know what's the number one industry in Israel?"

David shook his head.

"Tourism," Samuel said.

David wasn't sure where this conversation was leading.

"And do you know that ninety-five percent of our tourists are Christians wanting to see their 'sacred' sites?" David could feel the beat of his heart in his sweaty palms.

Mr. Cohen continued, "It's hard to imagine that many misguided souls."

David wrestled with the voice inside him. *I can't say*

that, he reasoned. They'll throw me out. Still, a scripture he learned in Sunday school came to mind. *For I am not ashamed of the gospel of Christ for it is the power of God unto salvation, to the Jew first and also to the Greek.* He met Samuel eye to eye. "Did you ever wonder what if they're not misguided?" Did he actually say that aloud? He prepared for the wrath of the man sitting next to him.

Instead, this Jewish man looked up at the stars and after several seconds said, "My brother-in-law has been talking to a man named Jonathan Bernis. Have you heard of him?"

David shook his head, unsure where this was going. "No, I don't believe so."

At this, Samuel stared at him. "He is the president of The Jewish Voice. He, my brother-in-law, and I had lunch the other day, and I've not rested peacefully since."

David had no idea what this man was talking about, but he was thankful not to be thrown out of the house on his ear.

Tamara appeared at the door and beckoned them to say goodnight to the boys. Soon Anna was saying goodnight, and David felt compelled to take his leave at the same time.

"It has been an honor, Mr. and Mrs. Cohen," he told them.

"We're thankful you joined us," Tamara turned to Anna. "Both of you." Leaning toward her husband, she whispered loud enough for him to hear. "He is here in a strange land far away from family. You should invite him to your sister's tomorrow evening for the beginning of Hanukkah."

"Oh, no, I couldn't impose," David replied.

"Nonsense. My wife is right. You should join us."

Anna put him on the spot further, "Oh yes, David. You should go."

What was she trying to do? He thought he'd done well to make it through tonight, but another day of impersonation during a celebration he knew nothing about would be his undoing. But it would be rude to reject at this point. "I'd be honored," he conceded. "What time and where?"

"You can accompany us. We'll pick you up at your hotel around five."

David smiled. "Great. Shabbat Shalom." When David left, Anna had already disappeared. Unfortunate, because he had a thing or two to say to her. By the time he reached the corner, he was frantic, thinking about tomorrow.

"How did it go?" Aharon asked.

David pointed back toward the house and raised his voice. "What was that? What did we accomplish tonight?"

Aharon laughed. "I thought I just asked you that."

"Well, I'll tell you. I can't pretend to be a non-believer because I am a believer. And while I may have scathed by tonight, tomorrow all will be lost when I go to their relatives for Hanukkah. And for what reason? Why don't we just grab Aliyah and leave? Have you found her or not?"

Aharon raised his hand. "Stop. Did you just say that you're going to Hanukkah tomorrow?"

David couldn't feel more frustrated. "Yes. And that was all because—" He pointed at Aharon, his anger surfacing, "—your daughter made it impossible for me to say no. Why would she do that? Now, what am I going to do?"

Aharon started walking down the hill. Over his shoulder, he answered, "You're going to go to Hanukkah with the Cohen family."

David soon fell into step beside him, seething. "No, I'm not. This is ridiculous. Why would Anna do that? She must not have been thinking."

Aharon stopped and stared at David. "Anna is in intelligence—Israeli special forces. She knew exactly what she was doing."

David backed up a step. He saw the change in his guide's face and felt his air of authority.

"David, how do you know Aliyah will want to go with you?"

"I know, okay? I just know. What are we waiting for?" Aharon grinned, annoying David. "Why should I spend tomorrow evening with the Cohens and their family? They don't have anything to do with Aliyah and me."

"Listen to me. I've spoken with BJ at length and I've done my homework. You need to trust me."

David almost objected, but then he felt a strange sense of peace come over him. It calmed and provided renewed patience. He inhaled and exhaled. "I trust you."

"Good. I'll be over in the morning. We have to get you ready to attend your first Hanukkah."

David sighed.

Chapter Twenty

David awoke at two, four, and at six o'clock in the morning when he finally got up. It had been over two weeks since he had seen or heard from Aliyah, the longest two weeks of his life. He yearned to touch her cheek, kiss her, and hold her in his arms, but he would be happy just to see her or hear her infectious laugh. David picked up his cell phone and selected her entry, but this time Aliyah's peppy greeting didn't answer. Instead, the number had been disconnected. For a moment he panicked. He was no closer to finding her than at the beginning. He had arrived in Israel last Thursday. Today was Saturday. Things weren't turning out at all like he expected.

He dressed and sat on the balcony of his hotel overlooking the Sea of Galilee. Even though his heart ached, there was something about this place. The crisp dawn air revived his spirits. The sky promised sunrise with the illuminating shades of purple, red, and yellow. It reminded him of the sky over the grass where he and Aliyah had lain. Over the last few months, just like their song, they'd forgotten the world and life was perfect with just the two of them, spending time together, going to church, and trusting that all would be okay. Now, the world was closing in on them like floodwaters from a broken dam, and he wasn't sure how they'd emerge.

David thought about the Cohens—Samuel, Tamara, Rachael, Dan, and Jonathan. He admired their family, the beauty in their observances, and the playfulness of the boys. When Mr. Cohen had questioned the misguidance of Christians, how he wished he could have shared openly.

David stared at the sea. He sensed the presence of God and basked in the knowledge that he was looking at the very water that obeyed Jesus' command. Within his soul he clearly heard, "Be still and know that I am God." David made his requests known as the sun rose up in the east over Syria.

At eight o'clock, Aharon texted David to join him for breakfast in the dining room. When David entered, his Israeli friend was sitting at a table in the corner. Breakfast was buffet-style and, although David wasn't sure what he was putting on his plate, he piled it full.

"Shabbat Shalom," Aharon greeted him when David sat at his table.

"I hope so," he returned.

After the blessing, David spread his napkin in his lap, while the waiter filled his glass with water. A few ice cubes remained in the pitcher but none in his glass. "What's with the lack of ice here?" David asked. "The hotels don't have ice machines and they always serve water without ice."

Aharon finished chewing and swallowed. "In Israel, we conserve water." He scooped another mouthful without paying David any mind.

David took a bite of eggs. "So, what's on the agenda

for my education today?"

The guide dropped a heap of coins on the table, real ones and fatter fake ones. "Hanukkah gifts for this evening," he explained. "Real ones to be offered as charity and wrapped chocolate ones for the children." Then, he pulled a four-sided spinning top out of his pocket. "On Hanukkah, which is the festival of lights—" he began, but David interrupted.

"Yes, I know. I looked it up on the internet. In the second century, God gave the Israelites victory over the mighty Greek armies. The leader of the Israeli army was Judah, a Maccabean, who reclaimed the Holy Temple. When they lit the menorah, there was only enough oil for one day, but it miraculously burned for eight."

"What a scholar you are," Aharon quipped sarcastically. "So, you're ready, then."

David chuckled. "No, I don't know the blessings or any of the songs. Nor do I know the games. They're going to discover I'm not one of them and—"

The guide raised his hand. "Stop." He picked up the top. "This is a *dreidel*. Have you seen one?"

"Looks like a spinning top to me."

"You're close. The family will play spin the dreidel. The top of each one bears the Hebrew letters, *nun*, *gimmel*, *hei*, and *pey*. This is an acronym for '*nes gadol hayah po*' or 'a great miracle happened here.' The game is usually played for a pot of coins or nuts. Whichever letter the dreidel lands on determines who wins or loses." David squinted, and Aharon shrugged his shoulders. "What?"

"I feel like such an imposter. Last night, Mr. Cohen said something about the Christian tourists being misguided. I couldn't keep quiet. I asked him if he ever wondered if they weren't misguided."

Aharon stared at David. "What did he say?"

"He asked me if I'd ever heard of The Jewish Voice and a man named Bernis."

"Really?" Aharon's eyes bugged out. "He asked you that?"

"Yes, why?"

"Well, have you heard of Bernis or The Jewish Voice?"

"No. I was going to look it up last night, but I got stuck on Hanukkah and forgot."

"David, God may indeed be working in mysterious ways. He was talking about Jonathan Bernis, and The Jewish Voice he mentioned is a Messianic Jewish ministry."

David was shocked. Had he really spent Shabbat with a Jew who might be considering Jesus as the Messiah? David remembered how he'd sensed a prompt to say something but had refrained. "Seriously? I should have said more."

"No. You did right. For a religious Jew to believe in Yeshua often means he is ostracized from his community and even his family. It can, also, be dangerous. This is why we have to make sure Aliyah wants to go with you before we do anything."

David stared at him and contemplated the unthinkable. What if Aliyah had chosen to honor her father and mother? His parents told him it would come to her making a choice. He didn't want to lose her, but could the two of them be happy if she lost her family?

Aharon broke the silence. "Did Samuel Cohen say anything else?"

"No." David swallowed his last bite of breakfast.

"Wait. He said something about he and his brother-in-law meeting with Bernis for lunch."

Aharon nodded but remained silent as if deep in thought.

"What?"

"Nothing." Aharon glanced at his watch. "We'd better get started."

~

David studied his beard in the mirror. *Not bad for only two miserable weeks.* He placed the yarmulke on his head and started for the door. He passed the hotel clerk and nodded. *Victor must think it's weird that I've dressed differently these past two nights.* Once again, guilt crept in, pointing a finger at his deception. *After tonight, Aharon had better stop stalling. I can't wait to find Aliyah and put an end to these charades.*

He had only waited a few minutes when the Cohens arrived in a white van. The passenger side was empty, and David climbed in. He greeted Samuel, Tamara, and the children who sat in the back. Dan and Jonathan smiled ear to ear. Rachael blushed while acknowledging him. She turned and stared out the window.

"My sister's and brother-in-law's home is just outside the city. It shouldn't take us long," Samuel explained.

David nodded. "Thank you for including me this evening." The van made a couple of turns and then followed the road up a hill. The view overlooking Tiberias and the sea was incredible. From up here, the sky and water contrasted with the splattering of buildings. Houses intermingled with hotels and high-rises. Olive trees grew in abundance on the hillside.

"It's beautiful," David said. "The city's much larger

than I realized."

Mr. Cohen parked the car on the sloping drive of an expansive home, the same color as the others but much larger. Palm trees and other yucca plants dressed the yard. A young girl about twelve with a long black ponytail played outside, despite her dress and nice shoes. She ran to meet the vehicle. "Uncle Samuel and Aunt Tamara," she cried out and hugged each one.

"Deborah." Mrs. Cohen clasped her arms around her.

Jonathan and Dan wasted no time. They and Deborah ran off to play. David helped Samuel carry in containers with food. As they entered the home, they each kissed the mezuzah.

"Chag Sameach." A woman greeted Samuel and he kissed her on each cheek.

"David, this is my sister, Esther." Samuel turned to her. "This is David, the young man I was telling you about."

Her face beamed. "Chag Sameach, David, and welcome to our home."

"Thank you for having me." When he spoke, her reaction caught his eye—a slight shift of her head or a knowing glint in her eyes. He didn't say more because he hadn't asked the last name of the Cohens' relatives and didn't feel comfortable calling her by her first name. Esther's resemblance to Samuel was strong.

"Where's Yosef?" Samuel asked.

She relieved him of his containers and answered on her way to the kitchen. "He's upstairs. He'll be down in a moment."

David followed her and set his bag on the counter, then returned to the main room. The furnishings of this home were elegant. Across from the front door on the opposite side of the mezuzah was a brass table with decorative moldings. A silver menorah sat in the center.

Yosef appeared at the top of the stairs. "Ah, Chag Sameach, my dear brother-in-law," he greeted Samuel as he rapidly descended the steps. Everyone in the living room started talking at the same time. David couldn't keep up with the conversation or match their enthusiasm. Yosef hugged Samuel and kissed Tamara on each cheek. Then, to Esther he said, "Tell the children to come inside."

Samuel pulled David forward. "This is David from New York. He's come to celebrate Hanukkah with us."

Yosef nodded and shook David's hand. "Welcome. I assume you've met my wife."

"Yes, sir."

About that time Esther entered with the children in tow. "And my youngest daughter, Deborah. I have another daughter, but she's upstairs and will be down soon. You know how it is with women; they're always late." He chuckled and said something to Samuel in Hebrew.

Everyone gathered a little closer together. David's stomach turned flips. He couldn't have felt more out of place. They were bound to figure out he was not like them. It was a mere matter of time. What would their reaction be? He had come to like this family, but this was a waste of precious time.

Hopefully tomorrow, he would see Aliyah and discuss what she wanted to do. Then he could head back home for Christmas. How wonderful it would be to have her at his side, but he knew that would come with a price for Aliyah. *Oh, God, with you all things are possible. I need a miracle, Lord.*

As Yosef's and Esther's eldest daughter appeared at the top of the stairs, a frame on the wall caught David's eye. It was a picture of this new family a few years younger. His mouth gaped. In the photo, standing next to Deborah…was…

He lifted his eyes to the stairs and gasped. Her black hair was pulled to the top of her head, and curls cascaded over her silky-smooth shoulders. She wore a long, white dress trimmed in beige satin with splashes of glittering gold. She began her graceful descent. For all her beauty, and the excitement of the evening, she had no smile. Her sad, downcast eyes hadn't noticed him. She took one step at a time, emotionless.

He moved closer, and his movement caught her eyes. They widened and her feet faltered as she missed the next step. She tumbled down the stairs. Family members shrieked. David, closer than the rest, caught her in his arms.

Aliyah stared at him, blinking her eyes, as if she thought she might be hallucinating. He held her in his arms, not wanting to let go.

Yosef rushed to their side. "Aliyah, are you alright?"

She nodded, but her eyes remained fixed on him.

"I'm going to put you down now, okay?" he told her.

A gasp escaped her mouth at his voice. Everyone gathered around her, but she seemed to be in a trance. Finally, she acknowledged everyone else and started answering their questions about her well-being. She glanced down before looking up at him again.

Samuel came to the rescue. "Aliyah, this is my guest, David."

She shyly looked back to the floor again. "Welcome to our home, David. And thanks for buffering my fall."

"I'm more than willing to rescue such a beautiful young woman."

At this, her eyes ventured contact again. She was acting strange. Of course, she'd be shocked and perhaps as nervous as he, but there was something else.

There was a knock at the door and Yosef went to answer it. David hadn't taken his eyes off Aliyah.

When Yosef returned with a young man, Esther said, "Jacob, you made it."

"Aliyah just took a scary fall down the stairs," Yosef told their new guest. "We'll let her catch her breath before we start. But first, let me introduce you to David—" He frowned. "I don't believe I know your last name."

David noticed that look on Esther's face, that subtle gesture. He approached Jacob directly and offered his hand. "Hi, I'm David Andrew from New York. Here doing research."

"Hi, David. Jacob Steiner. What kind of research?"

Even though David was clueless on the subject, he welcomed the distraction of this foreign conversation. "Agriculture. It appears your climate here in Israel is rather similar to our state of Florida."

"I've heard that," Jacob said.

"And your produce is remarkable."

Mr. Zimmerman announced the beginning of the eight-day celebration of the festival of lights. Esther was still eyeing David. Everyone gathered in front of the menorah. Mr. Zimmerman sang the three blessings of Hanukkah in Hebrew: Blessed are You, Lord our God, King of the universe, who has sanctified us with His commandments and commanded us to kindle the *Chanukah* light. Blessed are You, Lord our God, King of the universe, who performed miracles for our forefathers in those days, at this time. Blessed are You, Lord our God, King of the universe, who has granted us life, sustained us and enabled us to reach this occasion."

David stole a peek at Aliyah who stood beside Jacob. Why wouldn't Aharon have told him he was going to see Aliyah tonight? Why would he allow both of them to be shocked like this? Now, here he awkwardly stood in the middle of her family and possibly her fiancé, pretending to be something he was not. The terrible feeling in his gut remained.

Mr. Zimmerman lit the candle in the middle. Then he used it to light a single candle on the far right. He then sang the *Haneirot Halalu* prayer in Hebrew.

Afterward, the family took seats around the room, all within sight of the burning lights. Different ones shared stories of past Hanukkahs. Aharon had warned David about this time. He listened attentively and laughed when appropriate.

"So, David—" Mr. Zimmerman began, but Aliyah interrupted.

"Remember," she yelled, "the time Dan punched the *Sufganiot* with his fist, and the jelly inside squirted all over my face?"

Both boys and Deborah erupted in peals of laughter. Soon everyone in the room was laughing. David had visions of Aliyah with bits of fruit filling on her cheeks, forehead, eyelids, and lips, and he couldn't repress a chuckle. Their eyes met.

Soon, Esther called them to the table. Aliyah helped by setting out the plates.

As David took a seat, Mr. Zimmerman asked him, "What part of New York are you from, David?"

Aliyah dropped the last plate onto the floor, and it shattered.

"Oh, I'm so sorry."

David rose to his feet and pulled the chair away from the fractured pottery. "Here let me help," he offered. Jacob Steiner remained seated.

"No, it's alright." She seemed flustered, but her obvious mishap kept him from the temptation of answering a question errantly. His middle name really was Andrew, but he'd been deceptive. Everything about this evening was deceptive.

Esther handed her a broom and pan while David started picking up the larger pieces. She swept the particles together, and he stooped to hold the pan for her. Their eyes met. How he wished he could talk to her. She shook her head slightly and took the pan from him.

David sat back down. It was a festive occasion with a table set with bountiful dishes. Around the table, all ten faces smiled, even Aliyah's countenance had changed. An air of blessings filled the room.

Jacob had taken a seat across from David, and Aliyah sat next to him. No one had mentioned that Jacob was Aliyah's fiancé, and David could only hope her family hadn't escalated things in that direction. Still, it wasn't easy sitting across from Aliyah and his rival.

Everyone enjoyed the fried foods, and conversation filled the air.

"The latkes are delicious, Mrs. Zimmerman." David's compliment was authentic. The potato pancakes were tasty. He became aware of Esther eyeing him again.

"Thank you, David, but your mother—isn't she a good cook?" Esther asked.

He glanced at Aliyah before answering. "My

mother's a great cook, but everything seems to taste so much better here in Israel. I only hope my parents have the opportunity to come sometime."

"If they do," Samuel told him. "You come with them because you now have friends here. We hope you will visit us."

"Do you have sisters or brothers?" Jonathan asked.

David smiled. "I only have a sister, but she's pretty cool. If I did have brothers, I'd want them to be exactly like the two of you." David winked at Jonathan.

As the evening progressed, they sang traditional Jewish songs. Aliyah's eyes met David's several times and she smirked as he tried to join in. At times, it appeared she was laughing at him. He almost laughed, too, but quickly sobered as he caught sight of Esther Zimmerman eyeing them.

The children and adults played spin the dreidel. He played with Aliyah, Jacob, and Rachael. Except for a one 'hey,' which meant he won half of the pot, he usually landed on a 'nun,' where he neither gained nor lost. Even though he couldn't talk one-on-one with Aliyah, being close to her and hearing her laugh made him feel better. He watched her closely with Jacob and convinced himself she was still as much in love with him as the last time he saw her. David spun and landed on 'pey,' which meant he was out. Soon, Aliyah emerged as the victor.

Many times throughout the evening, David noticed Esther staring at him with narrowed eyes—so often it was unnerving. Finally, the night came to an end without revealing his identity. The Cohens gathered their dishes, and everyone said their farewells.

"Chag Sameach and Shalom, David." Mr. Zimmerman held out his hand. "I'm glad you joined us.

Where will you be celebrating the rest of Hanukkah?"

David had thought about this question earlier and how he might answer it. If another invitation was extended, he needed to decline. "My guide during my research has planned for me to join him. Everyone has been most hospitable. I can't thank you enough for allowing me to be part of your family on this night."

"Shalom, David," Esther Zimmerman said with a tone curter than her greeting had been.

He kissed her on the cheek. "Shalom," he replied.

Twelve-year-old Deborah approached him, and he smiled at her. "Better luck next time with the dreidel," he said.

Aliyah followed, extending her hand. He clasped it as he gave her cheek a brief kiss. Something in her hand transferred to his. He stuffed it in his pocket, unnoticed. "Shalom, David. I think perhaps it's you who needs better luck with the dreidel." Everyone laughed.

"You watch out for those stairs. They can be hazardous to your health."

Jacob also said his farewells to the Zimmermans and David. As much as David hated to admit it, Jacob had been nothing but decent this whole evening, the perfect model of a good 'Jewish boy' for Aliyah. Surely it would be no match for the love he and Aliyah felt for each other. Had Aliyah told her parents about Jesus or *Yeshua* as Aharon called him?

Soon, the Cohens dropped David off at the hotel. Dan and Jonathan made him promise to visit them again.

Alone in his room, David pulled from his pocket the tightly folded piece of paper. He spread it out. Aliyah had written in her familiar handwriting, *tomorrow, two o'clock, New City Market.* David sat on the balcony in the cool night air and took a deep breath, savoring the thought of meeting his love after more than two agonizing weeks.

Chapter Twenty-One

His phone jarred him out of a dream. He tossed from one side to the other, eyes closed, fumbling blindly for his cell. *Who is calling me this early?* The cell fell to the floor, and his eyes opened wide. Aharon. "Hello," he managed.

"Good morning, Sunshine. Late night last night?"

"As a matter of fact, yes. You knew all along whose house I was going to, didn't you?"

"I did, but—"

David sat straight up and interrupted him. "How could you let me go to the Zimmermans' without a warning?"

In a calm voice, Aharon asked, "What would you have done differently if I had told you?"

"Uh…I'd—"

"You'd have worried even more than you did and talked yourself out of going. I wanted the two of you to react without any preconceived thoughts."

"Don't you think that was pretty risky?" was all David could think of to say.

"So? How did it go?" Aharon asked.

David exhaled. "Aliyah is meeting me today at two

at New City Market."

"Okay, that's good, right?"

David shook his head and frowned. "I still don't understand. Why dress me up and pretend I'm Jewish the last two days?"

"Look, David. Aliyah has believed in Yeshua because of knowing you and that's wonderful. Today, you're going to try to convince her to leave her family and return to America. It's a big decision—in fact, for her it's life-altering. I thought you should spend some time getting to know her family—who they are and what they believe before you ask her to walk away from them forever."

David didn't answer right away. "I know. The last thing I want is for her to have to do that."

~

Yosef woke early with a heavy heart. He slipped out of the house and walked up the road to a nearby field. His troubled soul had much to consider. He sat on a rock and watched the sun rise. Boats, mostly the ones carrying tourists, traversed the water. These tourists flooded the Galilee week after week, month after month, wanting to see the places where their so-called messiah walked. It was quite an industry for Israel. He knew that, but he'd never considered what it meant—that for two thousand years people had followed this false god—according to history, a blasphemer at least.

The followers of this blasphemer had caused his people, the Jewish people, to be criticized, ridiculed, scattered, and even tortured and slaughtered. Through the hatred of Christians, Jews throughout centuries had been blamed for the judgment and death of this one man, whom they claimed was the Son of God. And if he were truly the Son of God, how could it have been possible for man to crucify him on a tree? Yosef shook his head vigorously as if to shake out the tumult in his mind.

He remembered Aliyah's words, trying to convince him that Yeshu was the Messiah. Her words infuriated him, but she didn't cower. She spoke with passion, entreating him to listen. It was as if a fire burned within her.

He thought about the words of Jonathan Bernis. If they didn't go against everything he had been taught and all practical reason, he would be almost persuaded. Yosef admitted to himself that despite all of his efforts to obey and observe his God, his sins were still many.

He'd read Micah last night and this morning found himself searching for answers. *God, as I have broken your heart with my sins and transgressions, so is my daughter breaking mine.* He wept.

After everyone had left his home last night, despite it being the first night of Hanukkah, Esther and Aliyah argued in the kitchen. His wife berated her, "Do you know that young man?" Esther yelled at Aliyah.

He entered the kitchen but remained in the doorway.

"Mama, I told you, I didn't even know he was coming to dinner." Aliyah threw the drying cloth down and started to leave.

"You're not going anywhere," Esther told her. "You're going to stay here and answer my questions."

Yosef saw the tears in his daughter's eyes. "What is going on here?" he demanded. With a motion of his head, he instructed Aliyah to sit, and she obeyed.

"Do you not have eyes, Yosef?" Esther yelled at him. "Did you not see the way that young man looked at her? Did you not notice the change in your own daughter when she saw him?"

Yosef stared at Aliyah, and his mind raced. Ever since she had returned home, he had feared for her well-being. It was as if their admonishments had squelched the very life from her. On her second night home, she spewed forth a story that struck his heart like a sharp sword. Not only had she found this friend from her childhood, but she proclaimed like all those tourists to have found Yeshu to be the Messiah.

Although he didn't think about it at the time, Esther was right. She did change when she saw this young man. Afterward, she smiled and laughed and appeared like her old self. "Aliyah? Is this true?"

His daughter didn't answer but stared at the table.

Deborah entered the room, but both Yosef and Esther yelled, "Go to bed." She recoiled as if she'd been struck but spun around and left.

In a loud voice, Esther continued. "Yosef, his name is DAVID! He even lied about his last name."

"Aliyah, say something," Yosef demanded.

She raised her tear-drenched face. "Yes, he is David, and I love him."

She lifted her head in defiance and Yosef stared at her. "What have I done to deserve this? It is bad enough that you say you love this man, but you also have abandoned the faith of your heritage."

"I told you, we should never have allowed her to go to school in America."

He turned to Esther with his mouth gaping. "You're blaming me? She's your daughter. You should have taught her better."

At this Aliyah burst into tears and ran out of the room. Esther started to go after her, but he held her back.

"Let her go."

Esther yanked herself free from his hold. Her seething eyes burned into his before she, too, left the room.

He sought the solace of the living room, where he lit the menorah again and started reading the passages that Bernis had given him. By the time he went to bed, his household was asleep. He slipped into Aliyah's room to watch her sleeping, something he had done ever since she had been born. He stroked her hair and smiled, but his heart ached.

Now, after a night with little sleep, Yosef found himself sitting on this rock and watching the creation of a new day, thinking about his eldest daughter. He had no sons, but since birth, Aliyah had captured his heart and fulfilled his existence like he'd never expected. He loved and admired her vibrant spirit and dutiful ways. What a privilege to watch her grow up from her toddler days of bouncing around and experiencing new things. He would rather lose his right arm than lose his daughter. Yet, he feared there might be little he could do.

It would take him a while this morning, for he had many questions for God. *"Baruch atah, Adonai*—blessed are you, Lord. I have tried to raise my daughter in the ways of your teachings. I have prayed that she would observe and follow the truths of the God of Abraham, Isaac, and Jacob. When I heard she had become infatuated with this gentile little boy in America, I moved my family to Israel. For years, I didn't allow her to use the internet and sent her to the best school I could find." Tears flooded his face as he looked toward heaven, "How have I failed her and you, oh Lord?" For all he had done, she still found this young man, and he had come for her. But above all, even worse than that, she chose to follow Yeshu, the blasphemer. Yosef stared into the bluish-gray sky and cried out, “Why, why?” He sobbed. “Where have I failed?” And finally, he begged, “Please don’t let her leave.”

By the time he arrived back home, Esther was slamming drawers and storming from room to room.

“What is wrong?” he demanded.

She tied a scarf on her head. “You’ve been gone all morning and now it’s afternoon. Do you not care about your family?” she accused.

“Enough,” he yelled. “What’s going on?”

“Your daughter is gone.”

He turned to Deborah who was looking on, “Did she say anything to you?”

She shook her head. “She hugged me and cried.” Tears formed in Deborah’s eyes.

Yosef grabbed his car keys from the peg on the wall, and he and Esther wasted no time.

~

David contemplated shaving the growth of hair on his face. He thought about Jacob Steiner’s robust beard, but this wasn’t who he was. He wanted to be himself again. Seeing Aliyah last night sitting across from her, watching her laugh and play, lifted his spirits. He hummed the tune to “Chasing Cars” as he wielded the scissors and razor and transformed his face back to normal while anticipating seeing Aliyah.

The room phone rang while David dried his face with the towel. “There’s a young woman here to see you, Mr. Drake,” Victor announced.

“I’ll be right there.” He pulled his shirt over his head. *Who is it—Anna or someone else*? He exited the elevator and rounded the corner toward the desk. His heart raced. With her back to him, Aliyah watched the front door.

"Aliyah?"

She swung around. At the sight of him, she rushed toward him and threw her arms around his neck. "Oh, David." She held on tight and softly sobbed into his shirt.

His hand cradled the back of her head and grasped locks of her hair. Something was wrong, but to actually hold her, touch her, and feel her close overwhelmed him. In a moment, they parted enough for him to gaze into her deep brown eyes. With a desire born out of nothing but the pure need for his best friend, his soulmate, he kissed her. She trembled in his arms. He pulled away, remembering they were supposed to meet at the market, not here. "Is everything okay?" he asked.

She stared at him. "No, nothing is okay, except that you came for me and you're here. I missed you so much it was as if I couldn't breathe."

He pulled her back into his arms and sighed. "I had to come for you. I thought my world had come to an end."

"How did you find me?"

"Turns out I know a guy." He smirked. "Thanks to God, I would have moved heaven and earth to find you."

"And pretend to be Jewish?" She laughed. "I wish you could have seen your face as you tried to sing in Hebrew."

"Hey, I'll have you know I studied that. No one suspected, did they?"

Her smile disappeared. "No one except my mother."

"Really? I couldn't fool her?"

"It seemed to have more to do with me than you. She said I changed when I saw you."

“I’m glad I got to meet your mom, dad, and little sister. It was a glimpse into what makes you, *you*.”

Even though they stood together out of the way, people were staring. He pulled her into the hall by the elevator.

She reached up and caressed his smooth-shaven cheek. “What happened to the beard?”

“Why? Did you like it?”

“Nah.” She chuckled.

David stared into her gleaming eyes. “Oh, Aliyah, I love you more than anything. I know our path won’t be easy—far from it—but I can’t live without you.” He bent down on one knee and pulled a box out of his pocket. “Aliyah Zimmerman, my Jewish girl, will you marry me?” He opened the box to reveal the opal ring she’d declined all those years ago—a reminder of their first kiss.

Once again tears filled her eyes, and he freaked. “I’ll get you an official engagement ring when we get back to the states.”

She stood there, shaking her head. Her hands flew to her mouth. Had she chosen her parents over him? Would she marry Jacob Steiner despite her love for another?

“Aliyah?” he pleaded.

She nodded as a smile broke through streams of tears trickling down her cheeks. “Yes.” She laughed. “Yes!” Then she added, “DAVE.”

He didn’t care. Aliyah could call him whatever she wanted. When she held out her hand, he arose, took the ring, and placed it on her finger. Then he picked her up and swung her around, never wanting to let go. It was as if it were only the two of them, and no one else in the world existed.

~

Yosef couldn't help but be touched by the scene displayed in front of him in the hotel lobby. He'd halted and held Esther back. There he watched this young man go down on his knee. His daughter cried with joy and clung to the one she professed to love. Never had he seen her glow like that.

Then, as if breaking through a glass wall, Esther charged forward and yanked Aliyah out of David's arms. She spit on the floor at his feet.

"Mama," Aliyah shrieked. "Don't—"

"You filthy liar. You can't have my daughter," she yelled. "How dare you come to my house on a sacred day. Pig." She spit again.

Yosef watched, not knowing what to do.

"Mrs. Zimmerman, I—"

Aliyah struggled with Esther, "No, Mama. Stop." She broke free and ran back to David.

Yosef reached Esther and restrained her. "Aliyah? Is this what you want?" he pleaded.

"To bring shame to your family?" Esther accused.

"No, of course, not. If only you would get to know him, Mama."

"Hmph." Esther charged toward her again, but this time David stepped in front. "Please, Mrs. Zimmerman, I love your daughter."

Yosef grabbed Esther's arm and pulled her behind him.

David's eyes met his. "I would never harm Aliyah."

Esther yelled around Yosef, "You already have," she spewed. "You've changed her. She's not the same."

"Esther—"

As if he hadn't spoken, Yosef's wife strode forward

to his side and addressed his firstborn. "You are dead to me. Do you hear me? Go with him, but you are dead to your family."

Yosef grabbed his wife's arm. "Esther, enough!" In a last-ditch effort to hold onto his daughter, he turned toward her. "Aliyah, say goodbye and get in the car."

Aliyah shook her head before answering. "No, Papa. Please understand."

Yosef didn't blink the tears away while he burned the vision of his daughter into his memory as it would have to last him a lifetime.

"Mr. Zimmerman, please." Despite David's search for words, none came.

Yosef glanced at Aliyah's hand, firmly resting in the hand of this young man. He clasped Esther's, but she jerked it free. He pivoted and walked away.

They climbed in the car. He could feel Esther's loathing although they rode in silence.

So many thoughts flooded his mind. There was no disputing the love he had witnessed. His marriage to Esther was arranged. It was what was expected. Theirs was not a passion such as Aliyah's and David's, although he often yearned for that. Still, he had come to love his wife deeply. The early years had been filled with laughter and discovery. Now, they simply went through the motions of everyday life, and from now on, it would be without Aliyah. His heart broke.

Chapter Twenty-Two

The black sedan stopped at the curb of United Airlines check-in. David jumped out to help retrieve the bags from the trunk. The sun warmed the chill of the morning. With luggage sitting on the pavement, David helped Aliyah out of the car. It was time to say goodbye to a dear friend whose help had been invaluable.

"Well," Aharon said, "May the Lord bless the two of you with health, happiness, and peace." He kissed Aliyah's cheek.

When David offered his hand, Aharon pulled him into a hug.

"How can I ever thank you?" David asked.

Aharon patted him on the back. "I'll send you my bill." He laughed. "Be sure and pay it."

David smiled and shook his head. "Yes, but some things can't be paid for with money."

"How wise you are, young man."

"No, seriously, thanks for everything. I'm glad I got the chance to meet Aliyah's family."

Aharon nodded and pointed skyward. "Remember, God is still in control."

They hugged once again.

David glanced at Aliyah, and she reached for his hand. He smiled at Aharon one more time before turning and walking through the automatic doors with the one he loved.

~

Aliyah fastened her seat belt and rested her head on David's shoulder. "So, we're going to fly into New York and then drive to your parents' for Christmas?"

"Yep."

"Are you sure the dean is going to let me return to school?"

"That's what he told my dad, but only because you excelled in your classes."

She smiled but not for long. As the plane took off, she stared out the window at her homeland. Aliyah didn't know if she'd ever return, or if she'd ever see her loved ones again. David was her loved one now, but that didn't eliminate the void she felt. The great joy in her heart didn't abolish the ache in it. All she knew was sitting beside him with their arms entangled felt right. With him, she had the promise of a bright tomorrow.

Aliyah gazed at the ring on her finger. The diamonds sparkled around the translucent shimmer of the opal, her birthstone. This ring was symbolic of the first day David told her he loved her and the day he proposed.

David stirred and whispered soft against her temple, "I love you."

Aliyah smiled and met his gaze. "I love you too…Dave!" She giggled.

His mouth moved close to hers. "Oh yeah? And it's DAVID to you."

"Okay." Her lips met his. Their kiss lingered, as she savored this heavenly feeling. One day, they'd be able to wake up in each other's arms and just forget the world.

The End

Don't miss Melissa's Fate, first in the Fate Series

When Beth discovers the one she loves has deceived her, she flees New York City without telling him she's carrying his child. Two years later, she must return to New York from Connecticut to face her baby's father. Just when Phil decides to forget his love for Beth, she reappears with shocking news. He won't forgive her for what she's done, but he'll do anything to save the little girl he didn't know existed. With Phil and Beth at odds, nothing short of a miracle from God will change Melissa's fate.

Shattered expectations and unwitting mistakes drag this couple through the trial of their lives, a marriage of convenience, and ultimately a lesson on the importance of faith, love, and family.

Order Loves Fate third book in the Fate Series

To Deborah who lost her sister, Aliyah, to a Christian cult, the only thing worse than a Christian is an Arab one. But Amir, banished from his Arab-Israeli family, falls in love with the sad, beautiful, Jewish Deborah at first sight. A bond forms between them despite their religious and ethnic differences. Ever since Deborah's sister left, her parents, Yosef and Esther have loathed each other, and nothing can ignite feelings of love between them. While Aliyah and David return to her homeland of Israel, David's sister, Melissa, tries to reach teenagers with the sexual alternative of abstinence, but her own marriage threatens to derail her mission. Little do they all know what the God of Abraham, Isaac, and Jacob has planned for them and the Fate of their love.

Social Media

Website: www.DianeYates.com

Facebook: https://www.facebook.com/diane.yates.54

https://www.facebook.com/booksbyDiane/

Twitter: @DianeDYates

Goodreads: https://www.goodreads.com/author/show/4557439.Diane_Yates

Linkedin: https://www.linkedin.com/in/diane-yates- b0a95a15b/

Check out her blog: www.dianesponderings.blog

Read some of Diane's other books

Pathways Of The Heart

All That Matters

Christmas On The High Seas